AT
11 O'CLOCK

RAJ KASHYAP

INDIA • SINGAPORE • MALAYSIA

ISBN
Paperback 979-8-89961-171-1
Hardcase 979-8-89961-172-8

Contents

Chapter 1

At 10:50 am

— ✦ —

10:50 am:

I was sitting in a room that was about witnessing humanity's greatest achievement. The walls were white, with white tiles and cracks in between them. A window lets in the sun's rays. The room felt blue to my eyes, but those rays added a bit of an orange hue. People from all races were gathered here.

The room was buzzing with energy, and I felt my heart race in the midst of scientists, politicians, and journalists. I felt like an outcast among them as all of them were wearing formal coats, blazers, long coats, and pants in the formal colours of black, navy blue, brown, etc, and here I was wearing a light blue jacket over a white t-shirt and black pants. We were all eagerly waiting for the experiment to start, feeling that something remarkable was about to happen.

10:51 am:

A sudden realisation struck me – I was part of an important moment. I was here, watching an event that would change everything. Scanning the room, I felt a connection with the others who had gathered to observe this extraordinary moment. We were united in facing the unknown.

10:52 am:

The seconds seemed to drag on, each one feeling longer than the last. I glanced at the wall clock, watching the minute hand move slowly. There lay a machine that would eventually change human history forever. The hum of the machines filled the air, making it difficult to hear anything else. I felt I was on the verge of something incredible, my heart beating like a bird's wings, alive and rapid.

2 DAYS AGO...

"What are you looking at?" my friend Shubham asked me. In his black and teal t-shirt that read 'Chicago' and that he had worn for ages, he was scanning me as I scrolled down the entry page for the experiment.

"Umm… It's just… You know there is this scientist, Dr. Green. He has claimed that he has made a sort of 'machine' through which he can bend the fabric of reality." I answered him, but I knew my answer was not enough to make him stop asking any further questions.

"Fabric of reality? Reality is the fabric? How is that so?" He asked. His brows raised. He always has that one look on his face where he looks like a toddler trying to figure out what the difference is between a banana and an apple whenever I talk about space, time, reality, and stuff like that.

"Yes, very much like fabric. It's more like space and time, which are threads that make up a fabric called reality. I mean it's a vague explanation, but yeah, that's overall what it is." He surely had no idea what I just said, but he always acted like he understood.

He stared at me for a moment and began, "So this dude, Dr. Red…" "Green," I corrected. Yeahh… Green, whatever, is he going to like to bend them and squish them like a stuffed animal?" I wanted to correct him so badly, but I knew even if I started, he would probably forget about it after about fifteen minutes.

"Yeah, something like that," I agreed with him anyway.

"Okkkkkk. So, are you going there? Going to witness the experiment?" he asked.

"Yep, surely, I will. Only five high school students are chosen to witness this experiment, and I happen to be one of them. I guess all those pan-country competitions and science exhibitions that I have won may have some benefits." I look at the shelf where all of my trophies are kept. They are worthless to me. What is the point of having these shiny objects if humans cannot unravel the mystery of what lies beyond them? But humans are just weird creatures. Medals, victory, praises, and all these things make them feel good as if they have really done something. I just don't get those things anymore.

I looked at the frame, which contained a picture of me and my mom. If only I could bring her back. But that's not going to happen in this era.

"So, what is the time of the experiment? Steven," Shubham asked, even though he had nothing to do with it.

"Its… umm… I guess… At 11 o'clock."

The night came, and Shubham left. I live with my aunt. I never met my dad and my mom… They died in a car accident. Well, at least I am not in an orphanage. Aunt Lily has always supported me. She is the reason I was able to study and eventually become a genius, which everyone says I am. She lives downstairs. And I always lie in my room. It has blue walls with quotes from scientists like Einstein, Planck, and others. My room has a small bed and a study table where I do all my studies and research. "Well, I guess tomorrow is a big day for me. I don't know if I will be able to sleep or not. I have never felt so excited before in my life. Let's see what tomorrow holds for me." I thought to myself.

I was sleeping soundly on my bed. Suddenly, the door of my room opened with a huge slam against the wall. I woke abruptly. I didn't know what happened. The door was wide open, but no one was there. Was it wind? I didn't know. But I also didn't want to think about what had made the door open so abruptly, so I again lay on my bed and slept in the excitement of tomorrow.

PRESENT...
10:57 am:

The room's tension hit a fever pitch. The anticipation within me threatened to overpower me. The machinery's hum continued, making it difficult to hear anything else.

Suddenly, without notice, it happened. A bright flash of light blinded me. The ground shook, and I felt pulled in various directions simultaneously. I closed my eyes and tried to shut out the chaos, but it was useless.

As seconds ticked by, my heart raced. The room seemed to pulse with indescribable energy as if it too felt the experiment's climax. Drops of sweat rolled down my forehead, and my hands were slick with nervousness.

10:58 am:

A tremor ran through the floor beneath me, starting subtly but getting stronger. The room shook, and my fellow experiment volunteers clung to lab benches for dear life. I scanned the room, looking for the source of the quake, but everything was in upheaval.

My heart raced as I realised this was the moment we had all been waiting for, the moment that would change everything. Glancing around, I saw everyone else frozen, their eyes wide with anticipation, all focused on the machine.

Suddenly, the humming increased, and the ground beneath us shook as if an earthquake were tearing through the building. I stumbled backwards, fighting to keep my balance. Walls cracked and crumbled, and the roof seemed to cave in.

Amidst the chaos, the machine's noise drowned out screams and shouts. It felt like being stuck in a hurricane—a whirlwind of sound and movement threatening to consume me.

Through the mayhem, I glimpsed the machine quivering with blinding light. All those metal pieces reflected the room, and one big plasma ball in the middle glowed with a yellow hue, almost blinding everyone around it. Shielding my eyes, the heat burned my skin even through my arm.

The light grew blinding, and I fell to the ground, unable to stand. The world spun around me, and I sensed an endless fall into a void.

Then, with a suddenness that was almost painful, everything went black. The noise, the light, the shaking—all disappeared, leaving me in a void of nothingness.

For a moment, I floated in the dark, weightless and directionless. Slowly, I began to feel my body again. The ground beneath me felt firm, and I heard my own breathing, ragged and uneven.

10:59 am:

I felt a force that pushed me backwards as if a giant hand had slammed into my chest. For a moment, I felt like I was flying through time and space, weightless and confused.

10:59:11 am:

I slammed into something hard and cold. I was lying on my back, looking at the dark sky above. I fought to catch my breath, feeling like I had been hit in the gut.

10:59:28 am:

My eyes finally adjusted to the darkness.

10:59:59 am:

I felt a sudden, silence wash over me. The clamour of the experiment room, which had been ringing in my ears since the beginning of the trial, was replaced by a startling quiet. It was as if the entire world had stopped for a moment, waiting for something to happen. The machine was still humming and glowing, but its sounds were now remote and faint.

Chapter 2

The Engraved History

AT 11 O'CLOCK

I groaned and opened my eyes, met with an immediate headache. The world around me seemed like a bizarre mix of uncertainty. People dressed in heavy coats and hats walked by, each holding a strange stick. It felt like a scene from a history book, and I found myself right in the middle of it. It was an unsettling event.

Trying to get my bearings, I realised I stood on a cold, harsh concrete road. The settings had an ancient feel, reminiscent of 17th-century London. Everything—the buildings, the clothing—resonated with a bygone time, leaving me confused.

Despite the pounding in my head, I took in the strange scene. Cobblestone streets stretched ahead, and old houses towered on either side. The air carried a smell from a long-gone era as if I had stepped into the pages of history rather than a busy city.

My doubt grew with each step. Confused thoughts flooded my mind, and I searched for answers in the middle of this unfamiliar era.

People around me seemed unaware of my shock. They moved with purpose, involved in conversations I couldn't understand. The strange sticks they carried were now obvious as canes or walking sticks, adding to the oddity of the scene. It felt like an unintentional trip through time, a moment defying the logic of my world.

I was walking the cobblestone streets, with tall buildings creating long shadows in the fading light. The echoes of horse hooves on rough roads and the distant clang of metal from a blacksmith's shop added to an atmosphere that felt truly historical.

Every corner turned, every person glimpsed, added to the puzzle. The air buzzed with the spirit of a society long past, and I was an intruder in the annals of time.

Amidst this antique environment, a fortunate accident changed the course of my journey. I stumbled upon a man carrying papers. I crashed into his back, and all the papers in his hands fell down the rocky street. I sat down to pick up the papers. Papers bearing a name that echoed through generations fluttered to the ground—

Julius Caesar. Retrieving the spread paper, a chill ran down my spine. Engraved on those pieces was a name associated with literary fame.

The man whose journey crossed with mine looked like a vision from antiquity. Half-bald, adorned with a moustache and goatee, he represented an age caught in ink. It felt as if the pages of history had opened before me, showing William Shakespeare, the Bard of Avon.

"You're The William Shakespeare," I cried, awe and shock mixing in my voice.

With a nod, the bard confirmed his name, sans the unplanned 'The' that had slipped from my lips. "I am William Shakespeare, indeed, not sure of the 'THE' part," he said, a gloomy air surrounding him.

Overwhelmed by the meeting, I stuttered, "I'm a huge fan of yours."

"Fan?" He seemed confused, and why wouldn't he? Obviously, he didn't know what a 'fan' meant. But I didn't notice it as I continued.

"I've read all of your works—Julius Caesar, The Merchant of Venice, Romeo and Juliet, Othello, Day Summer Nigh…"

"Othello?" he interrupted, real confusion etched on his face.

"You don't know what Othello is?" I was surprised that the very author of Othello didn't know what Othello was.

"I don't think I have written that piece; you must have mistaken me for someone else, young man," he replied.

"No, you have written Othello. It's a play written by you that revolves around the story of Othello, a Moorish general in the Venetian army, and his relationship with his wife Desdemona…"

And so, I told the full story of Othello to the very writer of Othello himself. Now that's what I call an irony.

My excitement dimmed as I presented the complex story of Othello, only to be met with Shakespeare's puzzlement.

"This seems quite perplexing," he admitted, creating a conflict in the weave of my thoughts.

In a quest for historical consistency, I asked the bard about the location, "I am lost, actually. Can you tell me where I am?"

"It's London," he replied with a charming smile on his face.

And I was now more confused than ever. I may have never visited London, but I knew for sure it didn't look like this at all.

And then I asked the question that I really didn't want to ask: "What year is this?"

"1601," he said. His words struck me like lightning, and now I was clear that I was not hallucinating or dreaming. This was it. This was the PAST. Othello was written in 1603, and I was in 1601. "It was obvious that he didn't know what Othello was. But does that mean that Shakespeare wrote Othello because I told him about it? But I knew Othello because of Shakespeare, and if Shakespeare got to know about Othello from me. Then, who had actually written Othello?" All these thoughts rushed into my mind, almost making my mind burst out.

Standing at the junction ages, the basic fabric of reality seemed to break. The unsettling feeling between the familiar and the unexplainable threw shadows of doubt, creating a tale that rang with the haunting whispers of an age long gone.

The meeting with Shakespeare felt like a surreal dream. "I should take my pen and note down what you told me, your story was impeccable, just a second," and as he turned away, I stood in the middle of uncertainty.

He turned towards where I was standing, but "Mister? Where are you?" I was not there.

I opened my eyes. It was nighttime. There were stars twinkling in the sky, but I couldn't see the moon. I turned my head, hurting with pain. The wind rushed through my face as I lay on the wet road. The wetness beneath me indicated a rocky road. Attempting to sit up, I felt a sharp pain in my back, causing me to groan.

I took a big breath and scanned my surroundings.

I couldn't remember how I got here. One moment, I was in 1601 London talking to Shakespeare, and the next, I lay on this rocky road in the middle of nowhere. Confusion and fear confused my mind.

The air was wet and heavy, raindrops splashing against rocks, and leaves moving in the wind. The smell of wet earth and plants filled my nose. Stumbling forward, I tried to get my balance. Laughter and music came from a nearby structure, and carefully, I approached, wondering what kind of place would be open at this hour.

As I got closer, I realised it was a bar with windows lit with a warm yellow glow. Inside, people laughed and danced, and the clinking of drinks and music created a loud ambience.

Standing outside, I felt out of place and confused. I didn't know where I was or how I ended up here, and the lively mood of the bar heightened my sense of being lost.

For what felt like hours, I stood there, trying to make sense of my position. A strange interest grabbed me as I stood outside the bar, drawn by the sounds within. I wanted to go to the bar. The night was cold, and it felt like winter as due drops trickled on my hair. I pushed open the door and was met by a scene seemingly from another time. Dim lighting, burning candles causing strange shadows, old furniture with years of wear and tear. I knew, like the last time, this was another 'time', probably in the past.

People danced in the middle of the room, spinning to the tune of a fiddle. The air smelled of whisky and cigarettes, and a few drunk men snored loudly on tables. A bartender, with a thick beard and a dirty dress, poured drinks for guests.

As I went further into the room, my eyes caught the decorations on the walls—old paintings of landscapes and portraits, some broken and peeling.

This scene made me feel out of place. These people lived in a world so different from mine, one I had never experienced before. Yet, there was something strangely familiar about it, drawing me in.

Finding an empty table in the corner, I sat down. The chair creaked and was awkward, but that didn't matter. Lost in my thoughts, I tried to make sense of how I had ended up in this strange place.

Surrounded by the bar's noisy sounds, a man suddenly appeared and took a seat beside me. His sharp features and keen eyes struck me, and though I didn't know him at first, I felt his importance.

"A boy like you should not be in a place like this," he stated, his voice strong and powerful.

His comment caught me off guard. I mean, who was he to judge me? I was here for a reason I didn't fully understand myself.

"You don't know what's happening to me," I replied, trying to express the gravity of my situation.

"Really? What's the matter?" he asked, his eyes steady.

I paused, unsure if I could trust him. Yet, something about him made me feel like he could help.

"It's related to time," I finally admitted, not hoping he would understand.

Recognition flashed in his eyes. "Ah, I see. Well, maybe I can help," he said, a hint of joy in his voice.

Before he could say more, he paused, looking serious. "Oh, I almost forgot to tell you. My name is Nikola Tesla."

Chapter 3

Twinkling Stars

As I sat in the poorly lit bar, doubt rushed over me. Nikola Tesla, an outstanding creator himself, had just taken a place beside me. It was a strange event. At first, I hadn't recognised him, dressed simply, with messy hair. However, as soon as he spoke, there was no mistake who he was.

"A boy like you shouldn't be in a place like this," he stated, eyeing me up and down. His accent was thick, and he spoke slowly and carefully. His face was long, and he didn't have his iconic moustache, as he had in all of his pictures. He had wrinkles all over his face and scars, more like the testimony that told about his experience and wisdom.

I nodded, unsure of how to react, and he seemed to take that as permission to continue.

"Something tells me you're not from around here," he said, resting in his chair.

"You could say that," I answered, feeling a bit nervous. Revealing too much to a stranger, even one like Tesla, wasn't my goal.

"It's related to time," I added, trying to pique his attention.

His eyebrows shot up. "Time, you say? Fascinating. Tell me more."

I took a deep breath and started telling my story—my sudden ability to move through time and my meeting with Shakespeare in Elizabethan England. Tesla listened carefully, nodding occasionally and asking the rare question. When I finished, he rubbed his chin thoughtfully.

"Remarkable," he said finally. "If what you're telling me is true—and I have no reason to doubt you—then you may have stumbled upon one of the great secrets of the universe." And there it was. The genius himself. If I had told this to anyone else, they would think I am crazy or they would lose their mind. But here this man was just impressed. Nothing more, as if he knew that this was obviously possible.

Leaning forward, I was eager for more. "What do you mean?"

"Time is not what we think it is," he stated, looking me straight in the eye. "It's not a steady, linear road going slowly forward. Instead, it's flexible, like a piece of clay. It can be stretched and squeezed, bent and twisted. And if what you're saying is true, then you may have found a way to change it. You know like basic relativity of Einstein's theory."

I was shocked. The effects of what Tesla was saying were shocking. It meant that everything we thought we knew about time, from Einstein's theory of relativity to the idea of cause and effect, maybe fundamentally wrong.

"But how is that possible?" I asked, feeling overloaded. "What about Einstein's theory of relativity? It clearly says that we cannot travel back in time."

Tesla laughed. "My darling kid, Einstein's ideas are just the beginning. They're just a child's scribbles compared to what we may find if we properly understand the nature of time."

He was right. Humans have not even discovered a tiny fraction of the universe's mysteries and yet we tend to drive the universe with our mere theories and assumptions. Tesla offered information about his study with high-frequency alternating currents, and I explained my thoughts on how my abrupt time travel may be related to my brain's electrical activity.

As we began our chat, Tesla, with his great intelligence, tried to understand the subtleties of my experiences. I recalled my jumps from one timeline to another, the lack of control over my locations, and the random nature of my excursions.

"So, you're saying you've been pulled through time and space without any control over your destination?" Tesla clarified.

"Yes, exactly," I agreed. "It's like I'm being transported through different times, and I have no idea where I'll end up next."

Tesla considered for a time, scratching his chin. "This is truly an interesting event. I've read of similar events in the past, but they were never properly explained."

Leaning closer, hungry for further understanding, I questioned, "What did you read about it? Who else has explored time travel?"

Tesla took a deep breath, prepared to share his knowledge. "Albert Einstein's theory of relativity has greatly changed the study of time. His study of the link between time and space has produced a profound comprehension of time itself."

I listened closely as Tesla continued. "What's amazing about your situation is that you seem to be experiencing something outside our existing idea of time. You're bouncing across timelines, assuming the presence of parallel worlds or alternative eras that cohabit with our own. Maybe it is superpositioning."

"Super positioning? What is that?" I asked.

"Okay, young man, let's have a conversation about superposition! Think about a toy that you enjoy playing with, such as a ball. It is safe to assume that you are aware of the exact location of the ball when you leave it on the floor. Only one place contains it. What if, however, your ball could be in two different places at the same time? Here we have a superposition. It's almost like magic, but properly speaking, it's a notion in science, especially in the field of physics.

In the enormous world of small things called atoms, they may act in odd ways. They are not limited to being in a single place; rather, they are able to be in multiple locations at the same time! In other words, it is the same as having your ball on the floor and on your bed at the same time.

This happens because small objects, like atoms and particles, don't necessarily follow the same rules as big things we meet daily. They can appear in numerous states all at once until someone or anything measures or sees them, and then they 'decide' to be in one single state.

Imagine that you have a magic coin that, until you really look at it, can be either heads or tails at the same time. This is how you should think about it. It's only when you look at it that it chooses to be either heads or tails.

Superposition is a weird idea, yet it helps scientists understand the bizarre behaviour of the tiniest building components of our world. It's like a puzzle that scientists are continually trying to solve."

I sat back, absorbing the facts. "That's a lot to take in. But why me? Why am I feeling this?"

Tesla leaned forward again, his eyes shining with interest. "That's the million-dollar question, isn't it? I can't tell you why this is happening specifically to you. To be honest, no one can. There can be many theories, maybe related to your DNA or cosmic rays or anything like literally anything, 'cause we barely understand superposition for small particles, let alone an entire boy."

We looked further into the secrets of time, investigating many hypotheses and tests performed over the years, from the classic clock experiment to current research addressing the impact of gravity on time.

As the night went on, I knew I was in the company of a great genius. Tesla's discoveries and ideas about time were mind-boggling, and I felt blessed to learn from him.

"Oh, my drink! I need to buy a new one. Would you want to have one?" he questioned, aware that someone my age shouldn't be drinking.

But a chance to enjoy a drink with 'The Father of Electricity' doesn't come every day. So, I said, "Sure."

"Great," he said and turned back and shouted, "Two cups of KK Burton, please." He turned towards me. What would you prefer, young man? Where is he?"

Silence, just silence, and a voice reciting:

Twinkle, twinkle, little star,

Once you shone, oh, how you marred!

Amidst this dark and vengeful night,

I shall unleash my burning spite.

Sorrow weaves its heavy cloak,

As whispered tears my spirit choke.

Bereft of joy, devoid of glee,

A wretched soul, now seeking plea.

Anger seethes within my veins,

Fuelling fires of righteous disdain.

Betrayal's sting, a poisoned dart,

Ignites a rage deep in my heart.

Guilt, oh guilt, a burden borne,

A weight that can't be left forlorn.

For in this tale of shattered trust,

Lies the truth of my sins unjust.

Revenge, my muse, now takes the stage,

Guiding hands on this vengeful page.

With every breath, I plot and scheme,

To quench the thirst, a blood-soaked dream.

Twinkle, twinkle, little star,

Beware the wrath that now unbars.

The night unfolds, in shadows cast,

In this world,it is dark and vast.

I'll rend the heavens, make them weep,

As secrets buried long, I'll reap.

No mercy shown, no mercy sought,

In this dark dance of vengeance taught.

Twinkle, twinkle, little star,

I'll blot your light, no matter how far.

For in this universe so vast,

Your brilliance fades, a thing of the past.

Sorrow, anger, guilt, and revenge,

Bound together, until the end.

Twinkle, twinkle, little star,

Beware the soul you've pushed too far.

There were no breezes, no light, no peace—only a voice repeating the same haunting melody again and again and again.

I opened my eyes to find myself resting on a bed of sand. As I gently sat up, I realised I was in a totally different place. In a dark environment where I was, the scenery varied, including areas of sand, marble, rocks, ice, and more. Each portion seemed to belong to a different world, creating a weird and strange picture. What actually drew my attention, however, was the sky. It was black, decorated with strips of lights that painted the dark canvas in a way I had never seen before.

The site was cold, although no air blew. It was quiet except for the man chanting the rhyme. His words echoed in the distance, creating an unsettling sound that sent chills down my spine. I felt like I had walked into another dimension—an area beyond time and space.

As I looked into the sky, I noticed the lights were in motion. They danced across the black plain, putting on a fascinating show.

As I stood on my knees, looking at the fascinating sky, I realised that the sand beneath me was not just sand. It was a mix of different materials, each with its unique shape and colour. The entire environment seemed to be a mixture of various elements—rocks embedded with marble, ice holding bits of sand, and sand interwoven with rocks. Everything in this place was carefully mixed, similar to a cosmic drink.

Questions filled my mind about where I was and how I had gotten here. Was this another timeline? A different world, perhaps? Despite my best efforts, answers slipped me.

Determined to find some signs, I decided to explore the areas. The lights in the sky seemed to call me, leading my way. Following them, my heart raced with hope.

My journey took me to a big marble structure, adorned with detailed patterns and designs. It resembled a temple or castle, and the lights in the sky spread from within. Cautiously, I approached the door, my heart racing.

Upon entering, I met a scene even more strange. The interior resembled a maze, with various paths leading to different rooms. Each room featured a fusion of materials, representing the varied blend of the outdoor surroundings.

As I tentatively navigated the maze, an unsettling shiver crawled down my spine, followed by the ongoing beats of my heart. Unanswered questions hung in the air, and fear clung to my shaking body as I went deeper into the strange maze.

The road ahead stayed hidden in darkness, with only faint hints of light leading my way. The maze seemed to possess a life of its own, a thing feeding off my fear. Every single corner led to a bigger maze.

I could not feel or hear anything, anything apart from…

Twinkle, twinkle, little star,

Once you shone, oh, how you marred.

Amidst this dark and vengeful night,

I shall unleash my burning spite.

Sorrow weaves its heavy cloak,

As whispered tears my spirit choke.

Bereft of joy, devoi…

Chapter 4

The Abyss

The echoes of the strange rhyme still stayed in my ears; its disturbing words echoing through the depths of my soul. The maze I had just run from stayed clear in my mind, a bizarre picture of horror carved into my conscious mind.

I pressed my shaking hand against my cold hands, seeking warmth and security among the disturbing chaos that surrounded me.

I considered the meaning behind these strange experiences, desperately looking for a hint of understanding amidst the mysterious puzzle I found myself stuck in.

Time seemed to stretch and twist within this weird place; wherever I was, it had a blue-ish hue to it.

The dark sky and the weird ground further distorted my sense of reality. The air hung heavy with anxiety, the space was quiet, broken only by the faint echoes of my own footsteps and the occasional rustle of sand beneath my feet. Every cell of my being yearned for freedom, for a way out of this confusing maze of doubt.

I closed my eyes, took a deep breath, and tried to find a bit of truth in the chaos. Images of Shakespeare and Tesla flashed through my mind, their faces going in and out like ghostly shadows. What was their role in this absurd story? Were they mere viewers, caught up in the same web of unexplained events, or did they hold the key to solving this mystery?

Lost in my thoughts, I took a cautious step forward, my foot falling on the cold, harsh stone floor. The hallway stretched forever before me, its twists and turns veiled in doubt. But I couldn't afford to be bound by fear or doubt. I had to push ahead, to uncover the secrets that awaited me within this maze of time and space.

With each step, I prepared myself for the unknown, ready to face whatever met me in this vast expanse. It was all quiet. The haunting rhyme was still being chanted in a man's voice. But where was he? And more importantly, who was he? Who was chanting the rhyme? And why was he chanting this rhyme?

The lights shaped like long strands in the sky, glowing with muted colours of red, green, and blue, and others started mixing together. The once-muted colours of the mixed scenery now stood out strongly as a white strand, creating a long white stripe in the sky.

Suddenly, a raven descended, perching on a marble pillar that stood in the middle of nowhere.

"What was a raven doing here? And from where did the pillar appear?" Questions rushed through my mind, but there were no answers to these questions.

I looked upon the eternal sky. The white strap of light ended just above the raven, which was sitting on top of a white pillar. The raven had a full, black, feathered body, a mid-sized, pointed black beak, and phenomenal shining eyes.

The raven set its intense gaze upon me, and an overwhelming feeling of realisation washed over me—it was not an ordinary raven. Its eyes held a wisdom that exceeded common sense, and I sensed an old knowledge living within its dark feathers.

"Human, you stand at the crossroads of worlds," the raven cawed, its voice echoing with an old, almost magical quality. "The chaos of time and space has picked you. The answers you seek lie beyond the veil, but the journey demands courage and understanding."

"How can you speak? And where am I?" I asked.

The raven's wings spread wide, and with a final screech, it took flight, disappearing into the light. The air buzzed with electric energy, and the surroundings began to shift and twist, creating a bizarre picture of changing landscapes.

Suddenly, the land started buzzing with energy. Electric sparks sparked out of the land; and blue sparks that consumed the land. My body burst into immense pain as they struck me. I fell on my knees as I felt the current run through my veins. I wanted to cry, but all I could do was scream while lying on the ground. My entire body screamed in pain as the electricity consumed it. Blood trickled down my mouth but I couldn't do anything.

Suddenly, the pain stopped. My eyes were closed, but I was still lying on the ground. The rhyme had stopped. I felt peace for a fraction of a second. I turned and lay down on my back. Staring at the sky, all I could see was a dark black sky and nothing else. I jerked my body and stood up. The pain was still there, but it was better than before. The blood that had trickled through my mouth earlier was not there anymore. Not even the droplets in my mouth. As I stood up and tilted my head towards my right, I saw something unbelievable in my mind. Far beyond me, there was a man. A slender man in a white coat, black shirt, rounded black goggles, black boots, and blonde hair. He had a long face and was sitting in front of a huge black Grand Piano.

"Was he the one chanting the rhyme?" the thought surged in my mind.

As the guy turned towards me, a sudden change in the atmosphere replaced the earlier silence with overwhelming fear. It was a feeling unlike anything I had ever experienced, topping even the horrors of the maze. Paralysed by fear, I stared at the man with a long, lifeless face and black round goggles that hid his eyes, projecting a disturbing void.

Silence surrounded us. Suddenly, the raven flew above us, its dark feathers mixing with the dark sky, almost camouflaging into the sky. The raven's cry broke the heavy silence, booming with a mix of warning and urgency. The man at the piano, devoid of sympathy or sorrow, pointed his finger at me and demanded, "Die," and a sudden spark of light flashed in front of my eyes.

Just as it fell upon me, I woke up.

"HUHHHHH! Where am I?"

I woke up in bed—a bed that was mine but not mine at the same time. The room was mine, but there was something different. It didn't seem like my room, though everything looked the same. I stood up, walked towards the door, and opened it. The stairs were just in front of the door, leading to the ground floor, just like my house. I walked down and reached the ground floor. It was oddly similar to my house, but something told me that it wasn't mine.

I walked past the lane of the house that led to the kitchen. In the middle of the lane was our memory wall where my aunt and I had put up our picture frames from various places.

"Now this feels weird," I murmured to myself. There were a lot more frames than I remember last time. And then I saw something.

"Disneyland 2019? Paris 2019, November? Kyoto, 2021?" Aunt had decided long ago that in each frame, she would write the name of the place and the year we visited it. But... we had never been to Disneyland or Paris or Kyoto. How were they here? And why were we in these pictures? I held my head between my hands to provide it with warmth, but I couldn't find any.

I went upstairs to my room, locked my door, and sat on my bed. "Even if this were a different time, how is it that there is a picture of Disneyland in the year 2019? We never went out of the country. We are just not that rich. How is that even possible?" All these thoughts flooded my mind when I suddenly heard a cracking sound on my window. It was just adjacent to my bed.

And there it was, the same raven that was in that weird place with a black sky and sandy floor. My heart throbbed as I saw him. But something felt like he was not here to harm me. I slowly approached the window, cautiously opening it.

"You are confused, right?" The words, spoken with a strange echo, hung in the air. I glanced at the raven, my eyes widening with a mix of awe and amazement.

"How are you talking?" I asked, my voice showing my doubt. The raven locked its dark, intelligent eyes on me, its very soul seemingly pulsing with old knowledge.

"Ahhhh, not again. First of all, there are many factors for me to talk about, one major factor being that I am WAY TOO SMART, and secondly, you should be asking about your situation right now rather than asking how I can talk. That's basic common sense."

The raven was right. Well, it still didn't explain how he talked, but knowing what's actually going on right now was way more important. What is happening to me? Where am I? Who was that guy in the suit? And what were you doing at that weird place?" I bombarded him with each and every question that came to my mind since… since… Ah, I even lost track of time since I was stuck in this whatever maniacal game this was.

"Jeez, that's way too many questions at once. Ok, let me make things clearer so you can understand better. You see, the reason for you to travel from one place to another, or should I say from one time to another, is because of your temporal aura. That is why I was able to find you. You must have heard stories about ravens and how they could travel between different realities, right? Well, that is possible because of our temporal auras."

"Temporal aura? What's that?" I asked.

"Oh boy, this is going to take me a hell of a lot of time. Anyways, imagine time as a big, invisible bubble that surrounds everything. Now, think of temporal auras like colourful lights inside that bubble. These lights show how time is different for different things. For example, your breakfast cereal might have a quick temporal aura because it gets soggy fast when you add milk. On the other hand, a big rock might have a slow temporal aura because it doesn't change much over a short time. So, temporal auras help us understand how fast or slow things happen in the big bubble of time around us. The example of cereal and rock was a bit vague, but that is the basic idea here. It's like looking at the world through time-coloured glasses. So we, the ravens, have a stronger temporal aura than humans. So, we can move around in different timelines of our own free will as we mould our temporal auras. This is how I entered the Abyss and learned human language over a span of... I don't know, maybe a thousand human years, but only a minute for me," he replied.

"The Abyss?" I repeated, still grappling with the odd discovery.

The raven looked at me with his sharp eyes and began, "Yes, Abyss. Ok, so envision a world beyond time's grip, where the borders between past, present, and future dissolve into a web of existence like how a spider's web's strands are attached to each other, the same way. The Abyss is that nexus—a place where numerous histories interweave, creating a fabric of endless potential."

As the raven spoke, I strained to understand the greatness of its words. The Abyss, a timeless Abyss, explained the weird events in my life. The flexibility of time and the existence of different realities were both awe-inspiring and frightening.

"Within the Abyss, the threads of existence are not linear," the raven stated. "They weave an intricate dance, showing multiple results for every choice, every action. Your short journey into the Abyss offered you a glimpse of this beautiful story."

My mind flooded with thoughts as I tried to understand the deep nature of the raven's talk. The entire fabric of reality seemed to be laid flat before me, showing levels of existence previously hidden.

In the middle of my deep thinking, the raven stated, "You are linked to the Abyss, more like connected to it.

It is a world where time is both a maze and an open field and you, Steven, are caught in its web."

"What is happening with me?" I implored, my voice mirroring the bewilderment that assaulted my mind. "What is happening to me?" I repeat, "What is happening to me?"

The raven cocked its head, watching me with an enigmatic glow in its dark eyes. "You just said it three times," it answered, a cunning undercurrent lacing its bird voice.

"Yes, I know," I answered impatiently, desperation staining my words. "But what is happening with me?"

"There you go, fourth time," it jokes, teasingly unaware of the gravity of my situation.

"See, I'm not in the mood for joking right now. Please tell me what is going on and what this place is." I asked the raven. "Well, this is by all means your home only this time, or should I say in this reality, you are a bit rich." The raven replied in such a calming manner as if changing your past life is really common.

"There on the wall downstairs are pictures. Pictures of places I have never been, but still, I am present in those pictures. Why? And how?" I asked as these questions were running through the nexus of my brain's neurons. "Weren't you listening to me a minute ago? I just told you, you are a bit rich in this reality, and rich kids usually spend the money of their guardians by roaming all over the world, so that's what you were doing." Your entire life becomes a wilderness of time and reality, and when you ask the only creature that knows something about all the stuff going on, this is the answer that you receive.

"Hey man, or woman, or whatever you are, listen to me. Lately, my life has been a hassle. I don't know what's happening or what I am doing in this mess. Help me, please." I begged the raven for his help. "Ok, I will, I will definitely help you, but first I need something." And I knew it, every novel, every movie, and every TV series has this one moment where the main protagonist asks for help from someone who knows what is going on in their life, and in exchange, that person asks a favour. Yuta from Jujutsu Kaisen, Thor from The Mighty Thor series, Thanos from Infinity War, all of them…

Wait a minute. Didn't I say protagonist? Then why am I thinking of Thanos at this moment? Leave it.

"I am ready. You may ask whatever you want." I said to the raven. "Well, I want… I want something to eat…" There was an utter silence in the room. No one said anything. As if time has stopped. "Eat?" I asked. "Yes, eat." The raven replied. I enquired again, "You just want food?"

"Hey boy, just because I can speak doesn't mean I am immortal. And why are you so shocked? Never saw a raven eating before."

"Aren't you going to ask me for a sacrifice?" I asked.

"No," he replied.

"Enrolling me into a school where you teach about time," I asked again.

"No, do I look like a teacher to you?" he replied again.

"No, but not even my eyeball?" I asked.

"Ewww, why would I ever ask for your eyeball? That is gross," he replied.

"My soul?" I asked again.

"Are you an idiot from birth or did you become one recently?" the raven replied.

"Ok, then what should I bring for you to eat?"

"Ever see a raven eating barbecue? No right? Go ahead and bring some biscuits or something."

And so, I brought some biscuits from the kitchen and gave them to him/her/it, I really don't know whether the ravens use pronouns or not. As soon as he finished up his meal, he opened his marvellous wings, which shone under the moonlight and jumped and sat on the window. "Come out," the raven said. "Out, now? Isn't it time to sleep?" I asked. "Did you just say 'T-I-M-E' to sleep? Come on now, don't waste my time and come out," the raven replied.

In the middle of the night, I was getting out of my own house as if I were a thief. I came out of the window and jumped onto the lawn. Thank God, even in this reality, Aunt Lily only built a floor. In the meantime, I might have stepped on the flowers that were Aunt Lily's favourite. Once I get out of this present mess, I promise I will gift her a bazillion flowers.

The raven and I started walking on the road in the middle of the night with no one around us. It was just me and the raven under the bright moonshed. There was an eerie silence on the road. On the right side of the road are the same houses as before. On the left, there were trees that shone under the light of street lamps and were placed evenly at every two metres. "Ok, so now tell me properly and clearly what is going on with me, and why am I in a different timeline?"

"Ok, so now listen to me clearly and know one thing—while I am speaking, you are not allowed to say a single word, is that clear?" The raven said.

"Yes, it is," I said.

"Ahh, you just said, I told you not to."

"But…"

"Now just shut up and listen. So, first, let me give you a brief introduction. My name is He," the raven said,

"He?" I inquired in my mind because I was sure 'H-E' was not a name.

"I know that I have a pronoun for a name, but it is what it is. Talking about your case then you must remember the time you went to the experiment, right? The experiment related to space and time; you remember it, right? At least say yes or no," the raven enquired.

"You only said not to say anything, but yeah, I remember it," I replied.

"Yes, you remember the time I told you about temporal auras. Well, everything in our universe has a temporal aura. Be it your cornflakes, a mouse, you, and me, we all have a temporal aura. So, when the machine exploded in the experiment, humongous radiation was released from it. A radiation so high that it triggered your temporal aura into fluctuating at different vibrations. While fluctuating, your temporal aura reaches a high energy level, and it teleports you into a different time, reality, or whatever. It is more like your very own superpower."

"How does it even work?" I asked.

"Well, in your words, what you call a 'timeline', even though it is anything but a line, every timeline has a unique vibration it is vibrating on. And every being on that timeline is aligned to that vibration which we call temporal aura. Your temporal aura fluctuates. And when that fluctuation reaches a certain frequency, you get teleported to a different 'T-I-M-E-L-I-N-E'," He, the raven, explained to me the very existence of my power in minutes. It took me some time to grasp all of the things that he just said.

"So, am I the only one who got the powers?" I asked.

"No, there are a plethora of people who got powers like you throughout the infinite timelines, but your case is the most unique one," the raven replied.

"Unique? And how is that?" I inquired again.

"See, the thing is that every time, every alternate time has a different temporal aura assigned to it. When a creature with a temporal aura not aligned properly to that time's temporal aura enters it, the 'timeline' tries to disintegrate that creature with its temporal radiations. Eventually, the creature's body can no longer sustain the burden of the radiation, and the creature dies. But in your case. When the external temporal radiation is high on you, your body's temporal aura fluctuates, causing your consciousness to transfer to another time. And that's why I came to you. I thought maybe you need my help or something… Well, I am kidding. I didn't come here to help; I came here because I found you and our powers really interesting," he replied.

"Interesting!" Well, my life is going anything but that. You know, sometimes people enjoy their time, but this time, frankly, it seems as if the "time" is enjoying me.

Chapter 5

Cradle of Time

"Ok, wait a minute, first of all, you said I belong to a different timeline, right? So, it's like I am a special of my type, right?" I asked.

"Special? No, no, no, no, you, my friend, are not special. You see, the time doesn't revolve around you; it never did. There are infinite 'timelines' for every single creature, from that weird guy you humans call Elon Musk to a small insect that I ate a few hours ago. Every single one of them has different realities. Among these infinite timelines, you are just a mere creature who somehow has some powers. You must have seen those videos on YouTube where they compare the size of Earth to other planets and stars. Wait a minute, your 'timeline' has YouTube, right?" said He.

"Yeah, my timeline does have YouTube on it," I replied.

"Yeah, good, so you see like all those stars and planets there are, infinite 'timelines' and your 'timeline' is just one among them," said He.

"So, it's more like a multiverse, right?" I asked.

"Multiverse? No, it is nothing like a multiverse." The raven replied.

"But you said that there are countless possibilities for every creature, that sounds more like a multiverse where there is a possibility for everything, isn't it?" I enquired.

"Ok, let me explain. Imagine a tree. A tree has leaves, and those leaves grow on branches, right? In the case of 'timelines', the branches are the alternate 'timelines'. And the leaves are the events on that particular 'timeline'. You and I are both just on a random leaf of a random branch on this entire tree. But now imagine a forest—a forest filled with infinite trees with infinite branches with infinite leaves. Here, every single tree consists of infinite branches, which represent the 'timeline'. Now, here every single tree is a special universe, and this forest in which the trees are planted is what you call the Multiverse." And there you go. The secrets of the multiverse, time, space, and reality are explained in a single paragraph by a raven named He. At this point, I want to write a novel explaining all these events.

"Hey, would you like to see something?" The raven asked.

"Something like what?" I asked

"Something like a Cradle of Time." And that should be the last thing to which I should say no.

The night was wrapped in a cloak of mystery as I walked beside He, the raven, through the quiet streets of the neighbourhood. Each step felt like a trip into the mystery of the universe, and my senses were at their peak, absorbing every detail of the strange surroundings. The houses stood like quiet guards, their windows hiding the secrets of any number of lives that were taking place within them.

Ancient stories were being spoken by the trees beneath the covering of leaves, and the stars were sparkling with stories that had not yet been told. Umm... I guess that was a bit too poetic. No stars were telling stories. Despite my best efforts, I was unable to understand the concerns that were roiling in my head regarding the existence of these places and my own presence inside this unusual world.

We reached a small bridge that was bridging a narrow sewer, and its concrete structure looked to be lacking in any particular importance. He signalled me to go under the bridge-like structure, with the goal of getting an answer, I turned to He, my feathery guide. "Why are we going under the bridge?" My question was met with silence from the raven, whose eyes seemed to be filled with a strange knowledge.

We began our journey beneath the bridge and into the shadows, where the moonlight had a difficult time entering. The air temperature and the noises of the night became more hushed. Standing beneath the bridge, He stated cryptically, "Nothing in this universe is perfect, and its rules are no exception."

With those comments, He took a feather from its wing and, with a rapid motion, put it into a small crack in the concrete. I looked in surprise as the feather went through the surface, leaving behind a beautiful blue light, like a river of brilliant energy.

"Come closer. Let me show you what truth looks like in its true form," He invited.

I was not sure what was happening. The feather just went through the concrete with a blue light, and then he went through the surface with the same blue light. Now I had to do the same. I approached slowly. First, I put my hand towards the surface of the bridge, and as previously, my hand went through the concrete surface. I closed my eyes and rushed through the wall.

A bright blast of light overwhelmed my senses, forcing my eyes shut due to its brilliance. "You can open your eyes," the raven's words echoed. Slowly,

I eased my eyelids open, greeted with a spectacle beyond comprehension.

I found myself floating in a vast space, surrounded by giant orbs-like structures, spherical structures bursting with blue flames. Each sphere released a mesmerising glow, throwing a dreamlike blue brightness across the cosmic painting. It was a dance of celestial lights, an eternal music that passed the limits of consciousness.

In every direction, there were an infinite number of these spheres. I felt a mix of feelings—interest, confusion, a trace of fear, and an underlying thrill that tingled through my entire existence. It seemed as if I had stepped into the heartbeat of the universe, a world where time, space, and reality synchronised in a cosmic dance.

The orbs, like bright lights, lit the surroundings in an amazing glow. Their flames created a melodic buzz that echoed with their movements. The raven glided smoothly into the vast expanse, its wings slicing through the currents of energy. Its dark feathers contrasted against the blue brightness.

As I drifted amidst the orbs, I stretched my hand, feeling the gentle warmth of the fires that formed these cosmic things. It was a physical touch with the wonders that unfurled before me.

I could sense the world whispering its secrets—tales of creation, echoes of old societies, and the flow of cosmic forces. It was a sensory explosion that surpassed the limits of the daily, a glimpse into the majestic design of existence itself.

In that moment, I was both a spectator and a part of this cosmic view, a wanderer in the vastness of the unknown. The raven restarted its cosmic dance, telling me to explore the beauties of this unknown world.

"What place is this?" I finally managed to verbalise the question that had been circling in my mind since the light show unfolded.

He answered, his voice booming in elegance. "This is the Cradle of Time. Well, this place has no name, so I just made that up by myself."

"Cradle of Time?" I repeated, seeking knowledge, as if my very words were vibrations inside the cosmic fabric.

He chuckled, a sound that rang like cosmic laughing. "Let me ease things for you. This is where the first time bubble was made, where the spirit of timelines took shape."

I nodded, trying to understand the immensity of what was before me. "And all these orbs, what are they? And what is a time bubble?" I nodded towards the thousands of luminous orbs surrounding us, each pulsing with an otherworldly brightness.

"Time bubbles, they're like branches of a cosmic tree I told you before, diverging and converging in the vast expanse of the universe. Every single one of them represents a timeline, an alternate reality."

"Why are they round like orbs? Shouldn't they be like straight threads? Like we call them timelines, right?" I questioned, confused by the spherical structure that defied the straight ideas of time.

"Ah, 'timeline' is an idea given by humans. Reality is far from what the human mind sees," He said, his words ringing with old knowledge. "Past, present, future— they are not sequential straight paths. Instead, they are all linked to each other, making a loop. And what do a group of endless loops make?"

"A sphere," I said, as I realised that their spherical structure was indeed logical.

"Bingo! Exactly!" He confirmed, a holy master teaching me through the mysteries of existence. "These shapes show the interwoven nature of time. They live in a spherical structure, interacting and affecting each other in ways beyond our knowledge."

As I absorbed the deep knowledge, I couldn't help but wonder at the subtle beauty of this cosmic cradle. The orbs pulsed with the heartbeat of existence, each telling a separate story inside the cosmic music. (Sorry, again a bit too poetic, but yeah, they were like that.) The knowledge that time wasn't a straight line but a spherical structure of infinite possibilities expanded my view of reality itself. The heavenly landscape urged thought, and I found myself caught in the glory of the Cradle of Time.

Amidst the cosmic breakthrough, a spectacle appeared that distracted my attention. One of the bright orbs before us began to change, similar to that of binary fission. It was fascinating to see each feature of the orb split into two unique orbs.

Unable to control my overpowering interest, I turned to He, my guide through this celestial expanse. "What's happening to that orb?" I asked, my gaze fixated on the growing show.

He followed my look, and a knowing smirk flashed over his avian features. "Those are different time bubbles being made, Steven. It's a constant process —the ongoing birth of new times within the cosmic cradle."

"But how are they created? What causes the creation of a time bubble?" I asked, a real hunger for information fuelling my words.

He said, with an air of cosmic understanding, "Time bubbles don't form magically. They are produced through a cosmic ballet of choices. Every single one of these bubbles has a story and an origin, and choices play a key role in their building."

Choices—the word rang over my brain. "Every choice made by a creature in their time bubble leads to the birth of a new one. It's a fundamental link—the ripple effect of choices resonating through the fabric of time. It's the multiple-world interpretation. Imagine you're playing a video game where you can make choices. Let's say you're choosing a character's outfit. You can pick the red shirt or the blue shirt. Here's what normally happens:

You pick red, the game goes on, and the blue shirt choice disappears.

But the Many-Worlds Interpretation says something wild:

You pick red, BUT the game also secretly creates another world where you pick blue. Both worlds exist, even though you can only experience the red-shirt world. This is how the Many-Worlds Interpretation thinks the universe works. It says that for tiny things, like electrons, there are no set choices. They can be in multiple states at once, like being both "up" and "down" in energy. When mere human scientists like in your world try to measure these tiny things, it forces them to pick a state, like forcing the video game character to wear a shirt. But according to Many-Worlds, the universe splits. One world has the electron 'up', and the other has it 'down'; the up and down are just examples for you to understand the point, which is that they are different. Both universes continue, even though we can only see the one where the measurement happened. So, the Many-Worlds Interpretation says there are countless universes out there, branching every time something tiny has a choice. In one world, you might have chosen chocolate chip cookies; in another, you went for oatmeal raisin (gross, I know). Here's the catch: we can't travel between these universes and can only experience our own branch. It's a mind-bending idea, but it's one way your so-called 'scientists' try to explain the weirdness of the quantum world!"

They were true, the scientists were true! Superpositioning, Schrödinger's car experiment, string theory—they were all correct! Unlike what Einstein said about time, this was different. We had a choice, and we surely had a choice, as every choice led to a unique time bubble.

"So does that mean we have free will? In that case, we can never see the future, right?" I asked the raven.

"Free will? Umm… yes and no." He replied.

"But you just said that our choices create a new bubble, which means we have choices, right?" I asked him again.

"Well, see, there was a guy in your time bubble, what was his name again? Einstein! Yes, it was Einstein; he said that you can see your future as everything that is going to happen is already decided, on the contrary, there were many people in your time bubble, like Bohr, Heisenberg, etc, who somewhat gave concepts that were similar to what you are looking at right now. But let me clear this up for you. To imagine what Einstein said, imagine you are walking on a road, it's the time of winter due to which there is so so sooo much fog that you can't see just in front of yourself, does that mean there is no road? No! There is a road, but you can't see it. You will walk on the predefined road but won't be able to see it. On the contrary, Heisenberg and people like Schrödinger basically said that you make the road rather than following an already defined road. Or simply put, wherever you go, a new road is created. But the reality is somewhat their mixture. Imagine there is a HUGE network of roads. Infinite numbers of roads are all linked with each other. But there is still that fog. You can't see the road in front of you and that is why you make walk into any road in front of you, but if I give you a light or a tool to see through the fog you will only be able to see the road in front of you, does that mean all other roads don't exist? Absolutely NO! It's just that you are on a particular road. The only difference here is that you are on all the roads at the same time. I know it is confusing, but your human brain cannot comprehend what is really going on, and I tried my absolute best to explain this to your small brain."

Now that was a lot to comprehend. My mind almost spun with these ideas. They were so complex yet so logical at the same time. Amidst the bright hues, a cluster of bubbles drew my eye, their luminosity gradually turning to an alarming shade of red. As I was looking at them, they started to disintegrate into small particles as if they were being destroyed.

Unable to ignore this cosmic change, I turned to He, my guide in this celestial journey. "What's happening with those red bubbles?" I questioned, my gaze fixed on the disappearing orbs.

He, the raven, regarded the cosmic scene with a sad attitude. "Those are time bubbles that are meeting their end, Steven. The loss of life for these cosmic creatures is a dramatic occurrence."

Perplexed yet interested, I tried to understand the forces that led to the loss of these dazzling spheres. "What causes the death of a time bubble?" I questioned the vast universe seemingly holding its breath.

He, with a knowledge surpassing the cosmic world, said, "There are various causes, but a repeated theme concerns the arrival of unwanted entities; especially, creatures from a different time bubble. When such creatures enter another time bubble and, in their journey, change the fabric of reality too drastically, the delicate balance of temporal energy becomes broken. The result is the dissolution of the affected temporal bubble."

It was like the thing that He told me earlier: a different temporal aura either destroys the creature or the time bubble itself.

In the strange expanse of the Cradle of Time, a disturbing shift entered the atmosphere. What had been a domain of amazement and wonder now bore a nervous atmosphere. I could sense the change, a disturbance that tingled the limits of my awareness. He, the raven, seemed worried, and I, too, felt an unsaid tension in the air.

As my eyes flew across the multidimensional fabric, I was faced with a scene that sent shivers down my spine. There, between the intertwined histories, floated the mysterious man who had been a haunting presence in my recent, unexplainable events. The dramatic contrast of his figure—a six-foot frame dressed in a white coat and pants, a black shirt beneath, and circular black goggles hiding his eyes—seemed to challenge the very essence of the cradle. His blonde hair framed a long face, a strange familiarity bringing traces of earlier experiences running through my head.

The memories surged back—a confusing maze, a piano, a white pillar, a sandy surface, and a beautiful sky with numerous lights—all leading to this moment. My body was paralysed since I saw him.

Silently hovering, the man emitted a haunting atmosphere, his presence throwing a shade over the bright timelines. He seemed devoid of expression, an unpleasant calm that hinted at darkness beyond the odd experiences I had experienced thus far.

The mysterious person in the white coat and goggles broke the eerie calm, his voice ringing in the unique atmosphere of the centre of time. "So, you are here. Well, I must state I am witnessing you for the first time here. Among all your many, uh, let's say 'types', you are the first one to arrive here."

What did he mean by my 'types'? There were more of me?

"Who is he?" I murmured to myself.

"What's the point in knowing who I am? You won't remember a thing that is happening here; therefore I don't want to waste my... uhhh, I can't even say waste my time because I just have plenty of it all around me. Nevertheless, you ought to go."

Before I could gather my thoughts or answer, suddenly, the man was behind me, a move so fast and smooth that it defied the rules of perception.

His hand on the back of my shoulder, he leaned in and whispered into my ear, "I promise I'll tell one of the next 'you' about who I am, but right now, I am not in the mood."

In the next minute, my body burst into a bright flash of light. It swallowed everything, swallowing my awareness until there was nothing but the blinding brightness. And then, just as suddenly as it began, the light disappeared, leaving me in a nothingness devoid of any sense of experience.

Chapter 6

Encounter

My eyes were closed, and there was this intense silence; my body felt like it was floating in the vastness of nothingness. Yet, amidst this nothingness, my thoughts resonated with questions created by the cryptic meeting with the man in the white coat.

"What did he mean by saying he saw me for the first time 'there'?" I thought, wrestling with the idea that he might have met different versions of myself. The idea of 'types' echoed in my thoughts, raising the unpleasant possibility of countless iterations of my existence meeting the unknown person.

"Could there be more of me?" I wondered. The idea that this mysterious man would share his identity with my 'next me' further heightened my confusion. How could he predict the rise of another version of me?

Suddenly, I was no longer floating. I felt the ground beneath me. A marble tile kind of texture.

I opened my eyes. There was a pale yellow ceiling right above me. I was lying on the ground. At this point, suddenly, going blank and waking up on the ground was becoming familiar to me. I managed to pick myself up and kept sitting on the floor. The floor was marble. I was in some kind of basement. There were things that I quite didn't understand. A box filled with machinery parts. A leaking pipe. A broken plant pot through which a small money plant was germinating.

I finally stood up on my legs. I roamed through the basement and picked up a dusty and old book. There was a pile of different books kept on a table. As I walked towards one of the shelves in the basement, I witnessed a small staircase leading to a blue steel gate.

I took the stairs and pushed the door. The door opened with a screeching sound into a room filled with chaos. Papers were lying all across the room. The walls were blue, but it really didn't matter what colour they were, cause all the walls were covered with loads and loads of paper all over them.

I entered the room with a bit of hesitation. If someone came in and saw me, they would definitely freak out. If I saw someone walking into my home, entering the room from the basement, even I would freak out.

I went towards a sofa in one corner of the room. Even the sofa couldn't escape the chaos of papers. I picked one of the papers, and it read something like "The law of the photoelectric effect." Now that was interesting. This guy, whoever he was, seemed to be interested in science.

Well, I didn't have the time to be fascinated by all these. I had my own bigger problems to solve.

But while I was roaming across the room, suddenly, the door opened. A man wearing a long coat appeared. His face was covered by a scarf. He wore a woollen cap on his head. I could only see his eyes. But from his eyes alone, I could figure out he was an old man.

What surprised me the most was that this guy didn't freak out after watching me standing on papers with some papers in my hands in his house.

"The kitchen is just behind the door behind you. You can get something to eat over there," he said. His voice was coarse.

"Umm, what?" I asked, confused. The man's voice had a German accent.

"You looked as if you hadn't eaten for days," he replied. And he was right. I hadn't eaten for days, and now I was literally starving.

"But, mister, who are you?" I asked.

The man came near a table and started putting his gloves on it. Then his cap and then his scarf. His face was finally revealed, and it is an iconic visual that reflects both intellectual brilliance and approachable warmth. The most prominent feature was his unruly, white shock of hair that seemed to symbolise the untamed nature of his groundbreaking thoughts. His distinctive moustache, neatly framing his upper lip, adds a touch of whimsy to his facial structure humanising the genius within. The lines on his forehead and around his eyes tell the story of a lifetime dedicated to unravelling the mysteries of the universe. "Well, I am just a physics professor, my name is Albert Einstein."

I couldn't believe that 'THE ALBERT EINSTEIN' himself was standing in front of me.

"You are... you are Albert Einstein," I said. He looked at me with a sense of sarcasm and said, "And you are lost, I assume. You are not supposed to be here. As I said earlier, if you want anything to eat, you can have it from the kitchen; otherwise, if you are interested in these papers, I will call you a psychopath."

I was confused; this was somewhat different from when I met Shakespeare and Nikola Tesla. Why was he so sarcastic?

"Why is that so? If I am interested in these papers, why would I be a psychopath? Are you not interested in them too?" I asked. He looked up at me with his eyes filled with wisdom and said, "No, well, though people do call me a psychopath, still, if you break into someone's house to steal a few papers related to physics and get arrested, that is foolish of you."

I couldn't disagree with him, but something was off. He acted as if he didn't value his own creations. "Why are you acting as if your research means nothing to you?" I asked. He sat on a chair near a wall and started to take his shoes off. The old, worn-out shoes—it seems like genius people don't waste their time on buying shoes.

"My creations and research will only be beneficial for the upcoming generations, not for the current world. This world in which I live is more interested in wars, politics, power and all but not physics." I dragged a chair and sat in front of him. If anyone can explain how time travel works properly, it is Einstein.

In a pumped-up voice, I started, "See, listen to me, what I am going to tell might surprise you."

Though Einstein didn't give a damn about what I said I still continued. "I am not from your time, I am from another timeline, time bubble, actually. I am from a completely different time and place. Years away from now. I saw things that were bizarre. I saw alternate time bubbles, met Shakespeare, Nikola Tesla, and then you.

I am jumping from one time bubble to another like a random event of probability."

Einstein looked at me with an expressionless face. He didn't say anything to me for a moment, and then he began, "You know when you said that you were going to tell me something that would surprise me, I thought you were going to tell me that my first wife is going to return after all these years. I was scared for a moment, honestly."

Really? I just told him I was from the future, not his timeline/time bubble, but he wasn't surprised. He didn't even ask me about anything related to my case, as if it were common.

"Are you not surprised?" I asked.

"Surprised by what? That you are from the future?" he counter-questioned me.

"Yes, I suppose?"

He sighed for a moment and then started, "Do you really think that you are the first traveller who came to me and said, 'I am from the future or a different timeline'? Kid, you are just another entity stuck in this loop of time," he said. And that was enough. I couldn't say anything. I thought that I was the only one who could time travel. I completely forgot that if there are infinite time bubbles with infinite possibilities, then for sure at some point in time someone would have created a mechanism that could make time travelling possible.

"Here, come with me," Einstein said as he stood up from his chair. He walked slowly towards the gate in the room, which led to the basement from where I entered this time. He opened the door and then went downstairs. I followed him as he had told me. I went into the basement. The basement was dirty as if no one had cleaned it for decades. Einstein took out a box from a shelf and slammed it on a table nearby. He started picking out items from his old dirty box. "You see, this is a smartphone," holding a smartphone in his hands, he said, "Though I don't know how to use it, a traveller like you gave it to me 7 years ago."

Then he picked up a book, "Ah, and see this," he read out the title of the book, " 'AT 11 O'CLOCK', such a weird title isn't it? A traveller who seemed to be a writer also gave it to me. He said that there was a part where I met the main protagonist of the story and told him about the concept of time. I just read the part where I was in the book. And he did a terrible job at explaining the concept of time."

He then took out a photo frame, which was dusty, and picked up a cloth lying on the table to clean the glass of the frame. When the frame was cleaned, he said, "There it is, here you go, can you recognise who the guy with me in the picture is?" I took the frame in my hands. But what I saw was unfathomable to my understanding. I was there in the picture with Einstein. A different 'me' was there. A 'me' who was not 'me' but was 'me' in this time bubble. If that made sense. I looked at him, and he gave me that look, which told me, 'You know nothing about this.' I was out of words for what I had just witnessed was something I couldn't comprehend.

"The entire purpose of bringing you over here was to tell you that if you believe you are the only time traveller who is meeting me, then I am sorry, but you are wrong about it."

This was all insanity for me. How can I be so naive to think that I was the only one who could travel through time?

While I stood there, I tried to process the fact that I wasn't the only time traveller who had met Albert Einstein. The weight of this cosmic truth rang through the basement. After a moment of quiet, I took a deep breath and looked at Einstein.

"Professor," I started, "thank you so much for telling me all this. I know it sounds crazy, but I need your help. I'm confused by all of these events and can't find my way out. You know how to help me get through this mess."

Einstein looked at me and shook his head as he continued to arrange his strange objects. "Time is a river, and each person must find their own way through it, I can't get in the way of someone else's journey."

I pressed, "But surely, with your understanding of the universe, you could offer some insight, a guiding principle."

Einstein stopped, his eyes showing a mixture of sympathy and stern knowledge. "The best lessons are learned through personal struggles. You're endowed with the gift of traversing time, and that means you have the ability to solve its secrets on your own."

Frustration crept into my words: "What's the point of being the greatest mind if you can't even help me?"

Einstein, ever the sage, responded with a quote that chimed with a deep truth: "In the dance of time, the steps you take shape the beat of your existence. A thought, no matter how bright, cannot dance the steps for another. To truly understand the music of life, one must learn to dance solo."

I sank to the floor, the weight of my time riddle pressing upon me. "Professor," I admitted, "I can't even figure out what type of time travelling I'm doing. Sometimes, it feels like I'm going back and forth within my own time bubble, and at other times, it's like I'm jumping into entirely different time bubbles altogether."

Einstein, interested by my confusion, leaned forward, his eyes reflecting wonder. "Different time bubbles? What do you mean by that?"

I took a deep breath, preparing to share the riddle that had eluded even the best minds. "All the time travel ideas I've come across they're kind of wrong. It's not a straight trip. I'm not just hopping between past and future events in a linear order. It's more complicated, and more confusing. I find myself in worlds where historical events play differently, where I meet variations of people I've known, and where the results are utterly unpredictable."

Einstein, absorbing my discovery, leaned back against a table, deep in thought. "So, it's not a mere movement along the line of time. You're travelling through a web of options, watching the branching of eras."

I nodded, glad that someone finally understood the complexity of my temporal situation. "Exactly! It's like every choice and action produces a new branch, a new reality. It's not about past and future; it's about the myriad ways the moment emerges."

Einstein, with the elegance of a master, pulled a sizeable, draggable board into our improvised school within the basement. The grinding sound of the board against the floor seemed to echo the complexity of the subject about to be revealed. His eyes, those windows to the deep ideas he held, carried a sparkle of enthusiasm as he took up chalk, ready to illustrate the complex dance of timelines.

"Let's delve into the intricacies of time travel," Einstein started, his voice resonating with knowledge. I'll guide you through three possible scenarios, each contingent on the circumstances surrounding your temporal journey."

As he sketched, chalk lines turned the board into a web of options. "Firstly," he pointed firmly, "the classical scenario: If you were to venture into the past and, say, kill your grandparents before your parents were conceived, you'd create a paradox. In this case, your birth is erased, changing the entire timeline."

Einstein transitioned easily to another area of the board. "The second situation is more complex. Even if you were to remove your grandparents, the main timeline stays unscathed. Your life is saved, but an alternate timeline sprouts into existence, where your family, as you know it, doesn't exist."

"The theory of relativity opposes this thought, doesn't it? You said that the quantum theories of alternate worlds are wrong," I said. It seemed that this version of Einstein did not entirely oppose the concept of different realities, unlike the one in my time bubble.

"I never said quantum theories were wrong. It's just that with the current understanding of the quantum world, we humans cannot generalise the entire universe. The quantum theories are not wrong but incomplete."

With a gesture, he moved on to the third part of his lesson. "Now, the third case adds a layer of difficulty. After removing your grandparents in the past, in the present, you exist, but your family does not. It's a timeline where your actions bear important effects, yet your personal timeline stays intact."

As I absorbed the mind-bending complexity, questions grew in my mind. "But can only one of these theories exist at a time?"

Einstein's smile hinted at the depth of time dynamics. "No, Steven. The circumstances surrounding your time travel decide which idea holds. Each possibility is not mutually exclusive; they coexist in the vast world of temporal options. It's not about one idea being true; it's about the nature of your journey and its impact on the fabric of time."

I found myself lost in thought as the chalk lines on the board made a mesmerising pattern, each line indicating a divergence in time. The basement, initially a place of chaos, now felt like a school where the secrets of time emerged in mesmerising complexity.

As I began describing my journey through time, Einstein settled on the floor beside me, a silhouette against the mess of papers. My story unfolded like an ancient scroll, each discovery adding a layer of complexity to the already intricate idea of time.

I spoke of meeting Shakespeare, the bard himself, in a time not bound by books but alive with the energy of his works. Tesla, with sparks of electricity lighting his surroundings, stood as a testament to innovation. The mysterious man at the piano, a spectre in a surreal world, added an eerie tune to my account. I travelled to a place beyond time, observed the Cradle of Time, and found myself talking with a raven named He.

The maze left an indelible mark on my mind. My journey was a fabric woven with meetings that defied the linear limits of time. As the tale developed, even Einstein, the maestro of theoretical physics, couldn't help but be drawn into the perplexing story.

Seated beside me on the basement floor, Einstein's features reflected a mix of confusion and surprise. He had envisioned timelines as straight paths, not as the vague bubbles I described. His gaze, usually penetrating, now held the weight of fresh confusion.

Einstein, the very definition of human intelligence, bowed his head, grappling with the discoveries. It was then, in the middle of our shared confusion, that he spoke, "In the vast cosmos of existence, understanding is a fleeting illusion, a mirage in the desert of reality."

Looking upward, as if ready to share profound thoughts, Einstein found an empty place beside him. I had disappeared into the riddle of time, leaving him alone amidst the scattered papers and the echo of temporal conundrums.

"Boy? Where are you?"

Chapter 7

Chronicles of Grief

Again, as always, there was darkness everywhere. My eyes were closed, and all I could do was hear and feel.

I lay on the ground with my eyes closed and enjoyed the sound of nature all around me. A lively and peaceful soundscape was made by the soft rustling of leaves, the happy singing of birds, the faraway laughter of kids playing, and the caress of the wind against my skin. I felt a soft warmth wrap around me, and the cool grass felt good on my fingers.

As I slowly opened my eyes, I saw a green and bright world. The tree high above me was covered with bright leaves that blocked the sunlight and made designs on the ground that moved. It took my mind a moment to figure out that I was in the park next to my house.

A rush of relief and amazement rushed over me. I sat up and looked around in shock. Everything that happened was real: the comfortable shade of the tree, the sound of laughter in the distance. The park was the only thing that was there. It wasn't a riddle, a maze, or a centre of time, just a park.

I had to hold back the laughter that was bursting out of me. It rang through the quiet park, mixing with the natural sounds. I threw my head back, delighting in the silliness of it all. "It was a dream!" I shouted to the heavens as if the world itself needed to prove this newfound truth.

The grass beneath me became my haven, and I lay back down, looking at the patches of blue sky peeking through the leaves. The warmth of the sunlight felt like a gentle hug, and a sense of calm washed over me. I closed my eyes again, enjoying the realness of the moment.

It was just a dream, a strange journey through alternate realities and mysterious places. I chuckled at the wild turns my mind imagined. Little did I know that reality, even in its simplicity, held its own secrets and wonders.

The laughter faded, leaving behind a serene smile on my face. I basked in the tranquillity of the park, glad for the everyday beauty that surrounded me.

I stood up, brushed the grass off my clothes, and started walking out of the park. The same road I had travelled countless times now felt like a fresh journey. Every step, every corner of the familiar path seemed soaked in a different light. The trees whispered stories, and the flowers painted the air with their fragrant tales.

As I walked, I couldn't help but notice the details of nature—the delicate petals of a growing flower, the music of rustling leaves, and the bright hues of the butterfly that flew by.

The laughing that had exploded in the park continued to echo within me. The silliness of the dream, the strange scenery, and the meetings with historical figures—all played like a lively movie in my thoughts. A single dream had managed to flip my viewpoint, and I found joy in the simplicity of the moment.

The sun made golden strokes across the sky as I walked the well-trodden road to my aunt's house. Each step reverberated with increased respect. I marvelled at the play of light and shade.

My laughing became a partner on this walk, a natural expression of the mirth that bubbled within. It was a laughter that accepted the every day, praised the mundane, and rejoiced in the sheer joy of life. As I approached my aunt's house, I felt a sense of thanks for the ease that life offered.

The way to my aunt's house opened before me, and amidst the charming surroundings, my eyes accidentally fell upon my old house. There it stood, a haven of memories and sounds of a past that I had carried within me. The house, seemingly untouched by the hands of time, wore the same friendly face that held the spirit of my youth.

The exterior, painted in a calm pink shade, glistened under the gentle sunlight. The windows, adorned with curtains that once moved with the sounds of family warmth, now stood still. The yard, a painting of vivid flowers, and the laughter of yesteryears called me with a melancholy hug. It was a picture frozen in time, containing the spirit of a life that had once thrived within those walls.

As I looked upon the house, a rush of feelings rose within. It was not just a building; it was a house that whispered stories and the quiet reminder of a mother's love. My mother, who fled from this world before I could weave my dreams and share my stories with her, remained in the corners of my heart.

A whisper slipped my lips, carried by the breeze, "Mom, I wish you were with me. I wish I could tell you the stories of my dream." The words stayed in the air, a quiet plea to an invisible presence, hoping that somehow, in the vast expanse of the universe, she could hear the sounds of a son's desire.

With a heavy heart, I continued my trip. Just as the weight of my feelings threatened to overcome me, a familiar voice, gentle and loving, broke through the silence. "Hey, stop running; otherwise, you'll hurt yourself!" The words, spoken with a motherly worry, hung in the air, and my heart skipped a beat.

I turned around, half-expecting to see a ghost from the past, but there was no one. The voice, a ghost of my imagination or a word from the universe, remained a reminder that sometimes, in the quiet areas of our hearts, the ones we love continue to speak to us, giving direction and warmth, even if invisible.

The whisper in the wind continued, and this time, it called my name. "Steven! Stop running!" My heart raced as I turned back, half-expecting a sign of the past. To my surprise, a small boy, lively in a red sweatshirt and white shorts, burst forth from my old house.

"I'm going to the park!" he stated, the joy in his voice ringing through the air. Following him, a woman emerged, wearing a green sweatshirt and blue pants, her appearance demanding attention. With a stern voice, she warned, "I said, don't run!"

For a moment, time stood still. The woman stopped outside the house, a shadow against the memories etched on its walls. And then, as if led by invisible forces, she turned around. The sight that met my eyes was beyond understanding—the most beautiful lady I had ever witnessed.

Her eyes, deep as the oceans, held the knowledge of ages. Her hair flowed, with its brown colour. My gaze fixed upon her, and tears welled in my eyes, uncontrollable and uncontrolled.

It was her—my mother. The woman who had left me, leaving behind an empty space that time couldn't fill. She stood there, a picture of simplicity and beauty as if the entire universe had plotted to join us in this brief moment.

I couldn't understand the feelings rushing within me. The ache of desire, the joy of meeting, and the weight of years of separation merged into a crushing wave. Tears streamed down my face, each drop bringing the unwritten stories, the unheard words, and the silent love that only a mother could give.

In that strange moment, the park, the old house, and the path ahead faded into insignificance. All that was left was the hug of a mother's eyes and the knowledge that, even in the realms of dreams, some meetings are timeless and eternally poignant.

As I stood there, in a past that felt more real than any dream, I couldn't shake the strong sense that this was not a mere fantasy. The grass beneath me, the swish of leaves, the laughing of children—all of it felt physical, based on a world I wanted to be part of once again.

My gaze focused on her, my mother, the light of my past. Tears welled in my eyes as a medley of memories played before me—the comforting songs, the warmth of her hug, and the shared laughter that echoed through our home. I stared, unwilling to blink, for fear that this fleeting moment might disappear like a wisp of smoke.

Suddenly, she noticed me, a stranger in her familiar surroundings. "Are you okay?" she asked, her worry sincere. She must have seen my tears. I nodded, wiping away the tears, my voice revealing the depth of feeling within.

Approaching me, she questioned, "Are you new here?" I quickly created a tale, saying that I came to visit my aunt who lived nearby. She pressed further, asking my name. In that moment, doubt gripped me, torn between the truth and the careful dance of time.

"Albert," I whispered, a name picked at random, a cover for the truth I dared not share. But she saw through it, a strange sense leading her. "Now tell me your real name," she demanded, her eyes steady.

Caught in the web of her gaze, I admitted, "Steven." A silence remained, filled with unsaid facts. She smiled, a knowing smile that crossed the limits of time. "I don't know how I knew you were lying," she revealed. "Even when my son tells a lie, he pauses just like you did. Mother's instincts, perhaps."

I stared at the eerie similarity—a son's lies, a mother's insight—sewn into the fabric of time. "My mother used to figure out whenever I lied," I admitted. She responded, "I'm sure your mother is a very smart woman." A lump formed in my throat as I muttered, "Yes, she was just like you."

A pause hung in the air as the weight of our unsaid truths settled. It was then that my mother, the one from the past, broke the silence. "Even my son's name is Steven," she shared, her voice tinged with a hint of interest.

My heart skipped a beat, and I responded, "Yes, I know." A flicker of confusion passed over her face, causing me to improvise. "You called out his name when you told him not to run." It was a hasty explanation, a fragile web of words hiding the complexity of time.

Leaning slightly, she asked about my mother's whereabouts. "Where does your mother live?" she asked. At that moment, I felt a pang of sadness, a storm of emotions that threatened to engulf me. "She's... she's gone," I stammered, my voice barely above a whisper. "She passed away when I was six." Tears welled in my eyes, the pain of that loss returning.

My mother's look softened, sympathy etched across her face. She wanted to console, to heal a wound she couldn't understand. I appreciated her silent understanding, but the truth stayed locked within me. There were things I wanted to share, to bridge the gap between the years, but the constraints of time forbade such revelations.

As a heavy silence lingered, the weight of my unspoken sadness, I pondered the fragility of love. Not everybody you love is promised to stay with you forever. The bonds we create, whether in the transient nature of dreams or the harsh reality of life, are delicate threads that may fray and break. Yet, in those ephemeral moments, love finds a way to etch its indelible mark on the tapestry of our lives.

As tears welled in my eyes, my mother softly reached out, her touch a balm to my injured soul. In that tender moment, she said, "Those we love don't go away; they walk beside us every day. Unseen; unseen, but always near, still loved, still missed, and very dear."

Her words rang with an otherworldly knowledge, a comfort that transcended the limits of time. With her hands on my face, she wiped away my tears, and for a brief moment, I felt the warmth of her love filling the void left by years of separation.

But as her hands stayed on my face, a surge of feelings overwhelmed me. My mother's touch, so deeply familiar yet impossibly far away, increased the pain I had tried to hide. The dam of my feelings burst open, and I began to cry even more.

Concern was written on her face, and she asked, "Are you okay?" I nodded, unable to express the complexities of my heart. "It's just... You look like my mother. She was also like you," I admitted, the weight of my words hanging in the air.

Her understanding gaze eased, recognising the layers of sadness I carried. "It must be hard for you," she said, a whisper of pity in her voice. I could only nod, the ache of loss echoing through my being.

Then, she said words that stirred a different kind of sadness within me. "I don't even know if my son loves me the way you do," she confessed, her vulnerability matching my own. Without a doubt, I told her, "He does. He loves you more than you can imagine."

A heavy silence fell between us, holding the weight of unspoken fears. Finally, my mother spoke, her voice tinged with a melancholy truth: "Sometimes I feel like he doesn't need me every time." In those words, I recognised the universal desire for confirmation, the quiet plea for comfort in the face of love's doubts.

As I faced my mother, I felt an urgent need to convince her of her son's love. My voice, bearing the weight of real feeling, broke the heavy silence that enveloped us,

"He does need you. He needs you when he wants to share his experiences, he needs you when he is stuck amidst the chaos, he needs you when there's no time for him to regret his past, he needs you when there is no light in front of him, he needs you when time doesn't run in his favour, he needs you when he wants to cry."

I paused for a moment, my head bowed, and closed my eyes, gathering the power to say the words that stayed in the depths of my heart. "I need you, Mom," I whispered, my voice holding a mix of weakness and desperation.

Slowly, I opened my eyes, only to be met with a terrifying scene that destroyed the fragile reality around me. My mother's dead body lay on the ground, bathed in a pool of blood. Her eyes, once filled with warmth and life, now stared blankly at the sky, her mouth open in endless silence.

The shock gripped me, leaving me motionless for a moment. I fell to the ground beside her, uncertainty and sorrow etched across my face. I held her dead form in my hands, stammering and screaming in denial, "No, not again! I can't lose you again!"

In my desperate attempt to turn the unavoidable, I tried to stop the bleeding with my bare hands. Her blood stained my clothes, a physical reminder of a reality I couldn't accept.

As I looked up, desperate for help, a surreal and terrifying scene played before me. The very fabric of reality seemed to crumble into ashes. Everything around me was in a literal sense turning into ashes. The road beneath me, the trees around, the grass, the buildings in the distance, the sky above, and even the clouds—all dissolved into a whirling cloud of grey particles.

My mother's lifeless eyes, once a reassuring presence, met my look, and even they bowed to the relentless dissolution. Like everything else, they turned into ashes, disappearing into the thin air that rang with the deafening quiet of loss.

In that haunting moment, a deep silence fell over the disintegrating world. As the ashes danced in the air, I clung tightly to the remnants of what was once my world. And then, breaking the eerie silence, a deep scream emerged from the depths of my soul. Tears streamed down my face as I screamed in pain, a primal cry echoing through the crumbling remains of the world around me.

In the middle of the breakdown, I cried out for my mother, for the fleeting pieces of a reality that slipped away like sand through my fingers. My voice, carrying the weight of despair, rang through the ashen void, lost and unheard in the cosmic chaos surrounding me.

As I sat on the deserted ground, engulfed in sadness, a familiar voice cut through the silence. "Was that a bit too harsh for you?" The voice repeated, weaving its way into my awareness. I raised my tear-streaked face to see the man who had haunted my dreams—the Keeper.

There he stood, a ghostly figure in his signature attire—a white coat and pants, a black shirt, round black goggles, and a mop of blonde hair. The enigmatic man looked down at me, his face unreadable, as if the weight of time itself lay upon his shoulders.

"You stayed there for a bit too long."

Chapter 8

At 11 O'clock

I was sitting on the ground, surrounded by the pieces of what used to be, as the world fell apart around me. Once the world was over, there was a strange silence that lasted for what seemed like forever. My mind was plagued by sadness as it tried to grasp how terrible the loss was.

It was very quiet, but then a voice that sounded very familiar cut through it. "Was that a bit too harsh for you?" The Keeper, the mystery person I had met at the beginning of time, stood tall before me. With his trademark white coat and trousers, black shirt, and round glasses, he gave off an air of distance.

I lifted my tear-streaked face to meet his look, my eyes swollen and filled with a mix of anger, helplessness, and confusion. "What did you do?" I screamed, my voice cracking with the weight of feelings. A sarcastic grin spread across the Keeper's face as he responded.

He lightly said, "I have no grudges against your mother. It was just a time bubble that I erased. Your mother was part of a bigger picture that I tore down."

Anguish and rage rushed within me. "Why do you need to cry for your mom? Anyway, she was not, you know, your mother; she was just another person from another time, bubb...," the Keeper mocked callously, ignorant of the storm of feelings raging within me. In a moment of burning anger, I stopped him.

"Who gave you the chance to remove time bubbles? There were countless lives on that time bubble that you erased just now. What about all of them?"

The Keeper's laughter rang through the dissolving remains of reality, his voice twisted with a chilling mix of success and mockery. His face, covered in a strange half-light, bore a grin that seemed to revel in the chaos he had organised.

"You truly believe these time bubbles deserve to exist? Look closer—really see them for what they are. Across countless worlds, history repeats its vile cycle—an endless plague of greed, lust, and hunger for power. Kings slaughter millions in the name of thrones made of bones, rulers burn cities to dust for fame, and men betray their blood for a taste of dominance. The darkness within mankind festers, thriving in every age.

In one bubble, a man known as Caesar's desire drowns an entire kingdom in blood. In another, a scientist breaks the atom, reducing towns to ash, and leaving shadows where children once played. Even in worlds untouched by war, people bind themselves to desire—craving wealth, power, immortality—driven by a hunger that can never be sated. Tell me, what worth is there in existence where the strong prey on the weak, where the circle of pain never ends?

And it's not just humans. Even gods fall to evil. In one thread, a God who swore to protect becomes a tyrant, ruling over followers with fear and fire. In another, a hero who once saved the innocent becomes a killer blinded by revenge. Time itself bends under the weight of these mistakes. The strings of reality are tainted, sewn into a tapestry of endless ruin.

I've seen the madness of endless possibilities—the foolishness of countless choices leading only to despair. The very idea of free will is a curse, a temptation that pulls all life into the Abyss. I am the only one who understands, the only one who can break the loop.

So, I will erase it all—every flawed life, every broken reality. A single timeline shall stay, perfect and unchanged. No greed, no desire, no betrayal—only order. Each breath, thought, and step will be planned to precision. I will create a world where peace is not an ideal but a law. A world where every soul moves as one, led by my will. No confusion, no suffering—only unity.

You call it tyranny, but I call it rescue. A flawless world made from imperfection. A world where life itself is an expression of my perfection. Can't you see? The chaos must die so the order can live. In the end, you'll thank me. All of them will. Even if I have to tear down every thread of life to make it so."

His words wove a fabric of fiction, describing an ideal realm—a holy bubble untouched by the stains of inhuman activities. He made a picture of a perfect world, built according to his whims and wants. In his eyes, he wasn't just a keeper of time; "I am a saviour, a God standing on the edge of heavenly rule over the endless time bubbles that spread like cosmic fractals."

As I stood there, my eyes locked onto his, a rush of anger coursed through my blood. "You're no God; you're a murderer!" The words came from the depths of my being, a furious protest against the audacity of his claims. However, the Keeper met my blast with an indifferent response, a dismissive exhale that seemed to brush off my charge as unimportant.

"Hhhh, you will never understand my purpose," he sneered, his tone having an air of condescension.

"Whenever I try to show any of your alternate personalities the bigger picture, none of you wants to see the broader canvas I long to paint."

Confusion marked itself across my face like a shadow. The truth sank in slowly—variants of me? Were there more versions of myself spread across the vast stretch of time, each meeting this evil Keeper in their own unique way? The finding opened a box of disturbing possibilities, casting me as a single thread in the complex weave of time, where countless versions of myself came across the fabric of existence.

The Keepers' tale hung in the air, a scary statement that echoed through the ruins of disintegrating reality. Before I could say a single word, his voice rose in an angry scream, blaming me as the hindrance that stopped his big plan.

"You are the reason that holds me back! I have killed you 8,45,693 times till now," he shouted, his words booming in the strange void. The huge number he presented left me briefly confused. My variants, spread across different options, had met the same fate, meeting their death at the hands of this merciless Keeper.

His irritation spilled forth with a rush of pent-up anger. "One by one, again and again, I have killed you with my own hands, but there, out in some time bubble in a different possibility, you arrive at the experiment I conduct, and you get your powers again and again and again."

I stood there, a mix of surprise and understanding washing over me. My life had become a repeating event in the flow of time, an endless loop where I got my powers through an experiment.

"Why don't you just listen to me?" he begged, his voice now tinged with panic, "And then your versions would not have to die, and my perfect world does not have to wait any further."

Amusement flickered in my eyes, a strange response to the silliness of it all. My versions, myself in different forms, had met this Keeper, only to meet their death frequently.

The Keeper lifted his hands, removing the glasses that hid his eyes. As the eyewear came off, his eyes were laid bare, showing a familiar face. "I am Dr. Daniel Green," he stated, a name that resonated through the halls of my thoughts. "The same Dr. Daniel Greene who did the trial in which you were present, and through which you and I reached where we are now. I became God, and you became a dice that rolls off to different time bubbles every now and then."

The recognition hit me like a cosmic finding. Dr. Daniel Greene, the orchestrator of the experiment that split time and reality, now stood before me as the Keeper.

The dice had been cast, and the effects spread across the vast length of time, joining us in an inevitable dance of fate.

"Why? Why me?" The question burst forth from the depths of my confusion. What had I done to earn the anger of the Keeper, to be caught in this complex web of time chaos? The air echoed with my plea, a frantic question seeking answers amidst the crumbling reality.

Dr. Daniel Greene, now unmasked as the Keeper, met my eyes with an intensity that suggested an old fight. "You and I are quite similar," he began, the gravity of his words hanging in the air. "Our Temporal aura is far more powerful than mere humans, and that's precisely the reason why you and I got these powers through our experiments."

The Keeper continued, revealing the crux of our connection. "Even if I destroy all the bubbles at once, the temporal radiation from your infinite versions will be so high that it will erase my existence from space itself. Just your temporal halo alone can destroy millions of time bubbles in an instant. Just imagine an endless number of you radiating the same temporal glow."

The weight of his words settled over me like a terrible truth. I was not merely a victim; I was a living cataclysm of temporal energy, an unexpected threat to the very structure of the Keeper's envisioned paradise. The Keeper paused, quite pregnant with the weight of his confession, before he gave the scary conclusion.

"I just need to erase you from existence, and then I could finally achieve the society I wish for."

The cold determination in his eyes spoke of desperate ambition, a belief that the elimination of my presence was the only key to opening his prized perfect world. As the truth unfurled, I found myself stuck in a cosmic chess match, a pawn in the Keeper's grand design, where my very presence posed an existential threat to his envisioned paradise.

The Keeper stretched his hands towards me, an ominous action that would soon show the depths of his motivations. In the open void of the Abyss, his finding began to take shape.

"When I came into the Abyss, I saw what this reality actually was," he stated, his voice echoing with a sad knowledge. Humans are the animals that crave blood, lust, and power—these are the driving forces behind their every purpose. They speak of love, yet a small scratch to their fears can drive these animals to unspeakable lengths, eliminating everything in their tracks."

His words hung heavy in the air, drawing a bleak picture of humanity. The Keeper continued, his eyes cutting through the fabric of reality. "Steven, they are not living beings. They are monsters. Monsters that will not stop until and unless someone stops them."

As the weight of his finding pushed upon me, a deep quote repeated in the nothingness, encapsulating the essence of the world's inherent selfishness. "In the tapestry of human nature, the threads of selfishness weave a complex pattern."

The Keeper's determination shone through as he stated his goal. "I have to erase them, even if that asks me to annihilate you again and again." The seriousness of his words bore down on me, an acceptance of a dark job he thought was his to perform. And in that moment, my entire body burst into a storm of temporal energy, eaten by the very forces that bound the fabric of reality. The Abyss swallowed me whole, a brief life caught in the chaos of the Keeper's brutal pursuit of a utopian ideal.

I woke up to find myself lying on the ground, the emptiness in my mind mirroring the sadness within. In that moment, I needed an escape, a break from the constant pain that seemed to define my existence. I yearned for peace, and an end to the endless pain. But then, a voice, soft yet deep, echoed in the depths of my mind, disturbing the quiet sadness.

"Those we love don't go away; they walk beside us every day. Unseen, unseen, but always near, still loved, still missed, and very dear."

The words, a balm for my hurt soul, told me that the pain of loss was joined by the lasting presence of loved memories. Even as I wrestled with the weight of my mistakes, the voice offered comfort, telling me to find strength in the lasting bond with those I had lost.

Yet, in the depths of my mind, a choice took shape. I couldn't save my mother, but countless lives in the time bubbles were at stake. I couldn't bear the burden of letting them all die. The thought of the Abyss and its cosmic fabric filled my mind, and with an uncontrollable jerk, my body responded.

As my eyes opened, I found myself standing once again before the mystery Keeper. I couldn't believe what had just happened. My body had just exploded into light, but yet here I was again standing in front of the Keeper. Astonishment clouded the Keeper's features as he questioned, "What? How is that possible? I just erased you right now. How are you still here?" Determination coursed through my blood as I pointed towards him, a daring statement in my eyes.

My body changed into cosmic radiation once more, and the Abyss seemed to call. In an instant, I found myself in a vast, empty desert. The weight of my experiences pressed upon me, but a fresh resolve stirred within. I waved my hand across the sand, and at one place in the sand, my palm went through, leaving the same blue light as it had done before when we entered the Cradle of Time from beneath the bridge. I once again poured my entire body into that part. This time, I was not in the Cradle of Time but in the Abyss facing the Keeper.

"Ahh damn it!" The Keeper screamed. Once again, he turned my physical state into cosmic energy. I woke up again, this time in a city of the future. There were buildings rising into the sky. I started walking, and again I fell into the same blue light, which this time was coming from the ground beneath me. And again, I was called into the Abyss. There he was, the Keeper. He killed me again. Then I summoned in front of him again, and again and again.

Again and again, I got moved to a different reality. Sometimes in front of the pyramids, in a sea, at a mountain cliff, in a jail, on a bridge, a school named TGS personally it was quite good, then a room where I was sitting in front of a laptop and countless number of places and all the time, I just said one word. and was somehow able to find the blue light and was able to come to Abyss.

"Again!", "Again!", "Again!", "Again!","Ahh, shit! Again!"

After showing up a hundred times in front of the Keeper and getting killed by him again, I finally teleported underneath a tree. For a second, I wanted to go to the

Abyss again, but I calmed myself down. The environment under the tree's shade welcomed me with a sense of calm. The play of sunlight moving through the leaves made a mottled pattern on the ground. Surrounding me, the bright greenery oozed a feeling of calm and a link to nature. The gentle rustling of leaves created soothing music that harmonised with the faraway calls of birds.

My feelings hit a peak, and with a loud thud, I leaned my head back against the solid tree trunk. The repeated question rang in my mind: Why was I unable to beat the Keeper's relentless assaults? Each meeting ended with me being changed into cosmic radiations, a pattern of loss that seemed unbreakable.

Amidst the peaceful settings, I sought warmth and answers. The fluttering leaves seemed to whisper secrets of the world, but the mystery of my situation remained. Again, it was a bit too dramatic. Nothing happened like that, and the rustling of leaves was irritating, to be honest. Just as I felt the weight of hopelessness, a familiar voice stopped my thoughts. "Need my help?" The words, a light of hope, floated down from above.

As I looked upward, the brilliant light quickly covered the figure, leaving a silhouette against the bright sky. Adjusting my eyes to the light, the form became clear. He, the raven, perched gracefully on a strong branch. A fresh rush of energy coursed through me. Now, with the arrival of the He, I felt a light of direction in the chaos of doubt.

He, sitting gracefully on the branch, looked at me with intelligent eyes, giving a sense of understanding beyond the human world. I couldn't help but feel a mixture of relief and interest. "Where have you been?" I asked, my voice showing both thanks and interest.

He, the raven, began to describe his recent trip in a different timeline. "Actually, I accidentally crashed into a different time bubble, and when I was about to get out of there, I met a female raven whose name was She. I was lost in her eyes. I tried to impress her but…"

"But?" I asked. "But she was hunted by a hunter. She was my 86th crush who was killed by a hunter."

Well, though I felt sorry for He for his loss, but still, I was not in the mood for listening to a love story, especially not of a raven.

He, perceiving my worried face, pushed me to share my own tale. I continued to retell the events after the Cradle of Time, my meetings with Einstein, the Keeper, my mother, and the various deaths of myself at the hands of the Keeper. Each word carried the weight of the emotional trip I had taken, and as I spoke, I could see understanding and empathy in He's sharp eyes. He, the raven, a creature of the cosmic fabric, listened closely to the details of my life across time bubbles.

With a heightened sense of expectation, I turned to He, seeking the answer to the puzzle that seemed insurmountable—the defeat of the Keeper. He, the raven, looked at me with a seriousness that suggested the importance of the job at hand.

In a grave tone, He recognised the extraordinary strength of my temporal aura, topping even the Keeper's formidable power. He then told me, "Close your eyes." I did as he said.

"Now focus on the cosmic energy around yourself, feel the strands of the cosmic fibre," He insisted.

"I don't feel anything," I said.

"Oh, will you shut up and just focus?" He shouted, almost as if he were angry with me.

He pushed me to focus more deeply, to delve into the core of the cosmic tapestry. As I committed myself to this mental study, a slow knowledge of something ethereal started to permeate my senses.

With my eyes still closed, He told me to open them. To my surprise, the world around me had changed into a spectacle of lively, glowing threads that were interwoven and moved in harmony. "These are the strings that have moulded reality," He, the raven, proclaimed.

Then, He directed my attention to a stone beside me.

"Focus on that rock, try to see its strings."

As I focused on the rock, I could discern the complex strings that bound its life.

"I can see."

"What can you see?" He asked.

"There are strings or threads-like structures vibrating at different frequencies," I replied.

"Just twist one of its strings," He urged me to adjust one of these strings. With intense focus, I picked a particular thread connected to the stone.

I did nothing but just feel as if I was holding the string. Then I bent my hand ever so slightly. It melted; the stone melted! It smoothly turned into water that soaked into the ground beneath. The experience was both bewildering and empowering.

He, the raven, watched me with assurance and said, "Someone has found something new, isn't it?"

In the middle of the heavenly show of cosmic threads, I turned to He and began to understand the magnitude of their meaning. "These threads," I began, my voice a quiet understanding, "they control the very essence of how things work, don't they?"

He, the raven, nodded in understanding, his eyes showing both knowledge and expectation.

With a fresh understanding, I continued, "The reason the Keeper could burst my body into cosmic radiation was that he was meddling with these threads, wasn't he?" The knowledge hit me with a deep clarity. The Keeper's ability to control the very fabric of my existence was based on his interference with the cosmic strings that defined my reality.

He's positive gaze seemed to support further study, as if pushing me to unravel the intricacies of these cosmic threads. He said, "Right now, you have just mended one thread. Imagine what you could do if you could control multiple threads?"

"I can possibly defeat the Keeper!" I exclaimed.

"Bingo! You are correct!" He replied.

"But there's a catch." There was a bit of sarcasm in his tone that told me I had to do something else rather than just facing Keeper now.

"What is it?" I asked.

"You see, the Keeper has been there for centuries in human years, so you know, you can't just face him right now," He replied.

"So, how long will it take to learn my power?" I asked, but the look in his eyes surely didn't say soon.

400 YEARS LATER...

"Ooo my God, can we just take a break?" I asked, gathering air to breathe.

"What, no, if you want to fight Keeper, you need to know how you can control atoms and subatomic particles. Otherwise, he will tear you down into pieces." He told me with a sense of concern in his tone.

"But even if he did, I will again be resurrected, right?" I asked.

"How many times do I have to tell you you don't resurrect? You see, every time the Keeper kills you, your consciousness travels to a different body of yours in a different bubble. And you have been practising for so long that your temporal aura in this body is way higher than any other version, so you have a better chance at winning. If you die, your consciousness will travel to another body of yours. You may think that you are the same, but your body will be a new one, and it will take the same amount of time to reach this level as it took till now." He explained all the details that he had already explained a number of times.

"Hmm, speaking of time, how long has it been?" I asked.

"Umm, I don't know the exact figure, but I guess... around 400 years?" He replied casually.

"WHAT! FOUR HUNDRED YEARS?" I screamed.

"Yeah, of course. What did you think of?" He asked.

"Then why didn't I age?" I asked as a plethora of questions came across my mind.

"Really? Is that your concern? Beings with higher temporal aura age very slowly, and that is why you have aged so slowly, but look at you, you now have a light beard and moustache as if in the midst of puberty." He laughed as he made fun of my beard.

"So, how long will it take now?" I asked.

236 YEARS LATER...(precise)

"Are we still gonna practice?" I inquired.

"Listen, you boy, until and unless the Keeper does not find us feel blessed," He replied.

"But now I ca..." Suddenly interrupting me, the entire world started to shatter into ashes, just like it did when I met my mom. Everything turned into ashes, and there was he standing in front of both of us—the Keeper.

In his same outfit as ever, he stood tall in front of us.

"My mother always told me not to say bad things; it brought bad omen, and I should have listened to her." The raven screeched.

"It's been a long time since I saw you, my dear Steven," The Keeper began.

"I don't wanna die; I am going. Bye," the raven said as he spread his wings and flew across the Abyss, disappearing into the black sky. The Abyss was here—the same sandy floor, black sky with multiple glowing lights in the form of threads laid across the sky.

Everything changed as I found myself once again in the dark and eerie expanse of the Abyss. The Keeper stood there, his face a mix of surprise and anger. It seemed that my return wasn't expected. Good. Maybe I could use that factor of surprise to my advantage.

"I hope you didn't have much inconvenience." I joked as the Keeper approached me.

"This ends now," He announced.

"It sure does." A smile spread across my face. I practised centuries learning to control the threads of existence; this was my time to put an end to all of this.

The Keeper laughed. "You think you can challenge me? I control the very soul of time."

He launched the attack, but this time, it struck with an unknown force. The Abyss rang with the battle of forces. In reply, I stretched my hands, moving the cosmic threads. A barrier formed around me, a shield against the coming burst of cosmic radiation the Keeper planned.

"You're not the only one with tricks up their sleeve," I answered, my resolution showing through.

The Keeper's eyes glinted with rage. "You can't escape your fate. The heavenly threads bend to my will."

But I wasn't ready to accept that fate. Not now, not ever.

Our argument turned into a cosmic fight. Threads of energy intertwined, making a strange fabric that echoed the fight for control. With each clash, reality itself seemed to shift and twist. We weren't just fighting in the Abyss; our battle went through time and space.

"You're a nuisance," the Keeper spat, shooting a swarm of temporal shots.

I ducked and weaved through the attack; every movement was planned. The cosmic threads responded to my will, making ethereal shields and deflecting hits. I closed the gap between us, starting an assault driven by the threads' power.

Blow after blow, we swapped forces that echoed through the ages. I struck with resolve, while the Keeper reacted with the confidence of one who thought himself a God. The very fabric of reality quivered under the intensity of our clash.

"You can't comprehend the magnitude of what I aim to achieve!" the Keeper yelled.

I smirked, "Your perfect world is nothing more than a tyrant's illusion."

Our fight continued a wild dance of forces in the Abyss. Each punch sent shockwaves through the void, causing temporal rifts that glimpsed into different universes. We crashed through moments in history—old societies, future worlds, and times untouched by human eyes.

Amidst the fight, the Keeper released a rush of cosmic energy, trying to overwhelm me. But this time, I was ready. I called the threads to form an enormous shield, pushing against the attack. The cosmic forces fought, colouring the Abyss with lines of vibrant hues.

"You can't win!" the Keeper yelled.

I gritted my teeth, pushing against the force. I smiled and said, "Oh really? And can you?"

With a burst of energy, I broke through the Keeper's attack, pushing myself towards him. Our clash increased, the threads weaving a tale of defiance against the tyranny of control.

"Why do you resist?" the Keeper sneered. "Embrace the order I bring."

"Your order is nothing but enslavement," I answered, every word punctuated by a strike against his cosmic defences.

Our fight reached a peak, the very heart of the Abyss shaking under the strain. In a moment of clarity, I understood the power I held, the ability to change the lines of fate. The Keeper, blinded by his desire for control, failed to understand the real nature of the heavenly forces at play.

As we met, I seized the chance. The cosmic threads responded to my order, merging with the Keeper's soul. I felt the resistance, the fight of his very being against the remaking of his fate. The Abyss quivered with the coming shift.

"You can't manipulate the threads," the Keeper snarled.

"But I can," I replied with certainty.

With a rush of energy, I rerouted the cosmic lines, changing the Keeper's thread. He felt it instantly. He stopped pushing against me. There was an eternal silence in the Abyss.

"Why? Why do you have to do this?" He asked.

"You can't just decide who will live and how they will live. They have a clear choice." I replied.

"Why can't you see? I could bring your mother back. I can create a timeline where she would not have to die and where you can meet her again. Why won't you want that?" Keeper asked.

"Maybe you could do that, but what about the infinite numbers of myself with their mothers? What about all of them? You think all the time bubbles as one, but they are not. Maybe they emerged from one another but are completely different; they are not your slaves. They are free. And you can't just seize their freedom," I replied, my words echoing through the Abyss. The black sky of the Abyss started to turn white as Keeper's existence started to fade away.

Reality seemed to rage against him as his form melted into bits of cosmic radiation. The Abyss pulsed with the success of his resistance.

As the cosmic storm settled, I stood alone in the Abyss. The threads hummed with the sounds of the fight, and I realised the extent of my sudden power. I could travel the cosmic currents, change fates, and form the very framework of reality.

The Abyss itself seemed to notice the change. The heavy darkness lifted, replaced by a serene glow. It was as if the cosmic threads were joining in unity, making a new story free from the Keeper's control.

I took a moment to breathe, to understand the magnitude of what happened. The cosmic threads hugged me, a testament to the durability of free will against the chains of fate.

In the silence of the revived Abyss, I considered the threads that bound us all—a delicate dance of choices, consequences, and the ever-present chance of change.

The Abyss spread forever, an endless area where threads of cosmic energy were interwoven in a dance of life. I stood alone, looking at the Cradle of Time that held the core of all histories, the repository of endless stories waiting to appear. The scars from the intense fight with the Keeper stayed, a memory of the sacrifices made for the goal of freedom.

In the silence of the Abyss, He, the raven, dropped smoothly to rest upon my shoulder. His eyes, reflecting the knowledge of ages, noticed the toll the fight had taken on my form.

"Seems like you had a hard fight," He stated, his words holding the weight of understanding.

"I sure did," I answered, acknowledging the difficulties faced in unravelling the Keeper's control over the cosmic threads.

He, perceptive as always, asked a question that stayed in the silence of the Abyss. "What will you do now? Will you rule the time bubbles according to your will?"

I considered the question, and the desire to impose my power over the dates. However, the lessons learned in the cosmic dance guided my response. "No, not that. I've learned what it truly means to protect. I won't control, but I will ensure that every thread in the big cloth is free to dance its own dance."

A thoughtful silence settled between us, broken only by the faint hum of cosmic forces. With a sense of purpose, I offered a quote that echoed the profound truth

I had discovered: "Sometimes, to protect what you love, you must be willing to sacrifice even the threads closest to your heart."

He, the raven, nodded in recognition of the depth of my understanding. I then asked a question that held the potential to change destinies: "I can mould any strings, right?"

"Yes, you can," came the positive comment.

A smile played on my lips as I examined the choices that lay before me. With an evil glint in my eye, I asked, "What are you thinking of doing?"

In answer, I shared my plan, a mirror of the caring effect that had shaped my own journey. "I'll do what my mother did for me. Take care even when things are at their worst."

I projected my own threads in front of my eyes. They were more complex than any thread I had manipulated by far. I started hovering in the air and changing the threads of my very own existence. They twisted and turned each and every thread of my existence to match a certain frequency. And then...

My entire body slowly started turning into bubbles. The cosmic bubble, the bubbles, bright and pulsating, combined perfectly with the time bubbles within the core of time.

I converted my entire temporal aura into infinite cosmic bubbles, and each of those cosmic bubbles merged with the existing infinite time bubble.

It was a union of fates, a testament to the connectedness of all threads in the cosmic dance. As the merger continued, I looked at He and spoke with a mix of gratitude and sadness, "I'll miss you, my friend."

The raven, knowing the sacrifice contained in this act of defence, cawed softly, a goodbye that echoed through the endless expanse of the Abyss. The cosmic threads continued their dance, creating new stories, and I, having given control, became a part of the perfect symphony that echoed through the fabric of existence.

And now I am part of every path. I was part of all the fights and all the love stories. I saw Shakespeare write Othello, Einstein understanding the story of relativity, a boy writing a book in his room, sitting on his grandparents' bed, and my mother with me in her lap.

I saw He, the raven, approaching another beautiful raven 87th time, but this time she wasn't killed, but she refused. Poor He.

And now you—yeah, you, the one reading this book—look around you. I am standing just beside you, going through pages of the story that tells you how my life changed.

AT 11 O'CLOCK.

9 798899 611711